STRANDED ON SPARROW

SPARROW ISLAND BOOK FOUR

RACHEL SKATVOLD

ISBN: 978-1-951839-57-4

Celebrate Lit Publishing

Celebrate Lit Publishing

304 S. Jones Blvd #754

Las Vegas, NV, 89107

http://www.celebratelitpublishing.com/

ACKNOWLEDGMENTS

As always, there are so many people involved in putting a book together and I would like to take a moment to thank them.

First of all, thank you to God for placing this story in my heart. The characters in this book have taught me so much about trusting Him during the storms of life.

Second, thank you for those who helped with the publication process. Thanks to my publisher at Celebrate Lit, Sandy Barela, for making this series possible. I so appreciate the amazing job done by my editor and fellow author in the series, Chautona Havig and my mother Joy Davidson, for helping with proofreading. A special thanks to all the wonderful authors in this series. It has been a joy working with you all so far, and your stories are so inspiring to me. Also, a big shout out to my sister, Jenny Davidson, for taking my author photo. You have such an amazing talent for photography.

Last but not least, thank you to my husband, John, my kids, my extended family, and church family for all your love and support. Also, I'd like to give a shout out to my beta readers, reviewers and loyal readers waiting patiently for the next book to come out. You all are such an encouragement and I appreciate you.

Blessings.

~To my sister, Jenny.
Hey Lady. Thank you for being a sister I can go to for advice, be crazy with, and talk about anything with. Watching you get married last year filled me with such joy. I'm so happy you found the right one God intended for you to spend your life with. Praying you both have a lifetime of love, laughter, and happiness together.

"What is the price of two sparrows—one copper coin? But not a single sparrow can fall to the ground without your Father knowing it. And the very hairs on your head are all numbered. So don't be afraid; you are more valuable to God than a whole flock of sparrows."

Mathew 10:29–31

"Who in their right mind invented high heels?" Natalia Diaz grumbled while unzipping her stylish leather boots to allow her aching calves and ankles to breathe. After standing for two hours, a seat had finally opened up, allowing her some relief. The air felt so good, she pulled her feet completely out to stretch her toes.

"Number one hundred fifty-seven. One–five–seven," a nasal voice called.

"Just a minute!" Lia squeezed her feet back into the boots and made a vain attempt to zip them up. The left boot zipped up like a charm, but the right one caught about two inches up and refused to budge. She jerked and pulled to no avail.

"Last call. Number one hundred fifty-seven." The nasal voice said again, laced with irritation.

Lia gathered her bag and made her way up, her right boot flapping around like a flat tire on the highway. She made it halfway before her ankle twisted sideways. Grumbling again, she yanked the troublemaker boot off and hobbled the remainder of her journey to the front desk. She slid the number across the desk with an exasperated chuckle. "Sorry, wardrobe malfunction, but I'm here."

The receptionist took the slip of paper but didn't look up. Instead, she kept a laser focus on her computer screen. "Name?"

"Natalia Diaz...but I..."

"Have you filled out the application online?"

"Yes, but..."

"What date did you fill it out?"

Lia bit her lip to keep from losing her temper. "About a month ago, but..."

"I need an exact date to look up your application."

She looked at her phone calendar, knowing it had been the first Tuesday of last month. She told her the date and waited. "I know the application was submitted, but I haven't received any calls yet. I wondered if maybe I put in the wrong number?"

The receptionist furrowed her brow and confirmed the number. Then she looked up at her with pursed lips. "Ma'am, everything looks in order. Someone should be in contact with you when a job comes available."

Lia shook her head. "It's been a month. If I can't pay my rent, I'll lose my apartment."

"I'm sorry. This is a temp agency. We help connect people with temporary jobs, but we can't work miracles. We can't predict when a job will become available either. You just have to wait."

A smart remark threatened to escape her mouth, but she held it back. "Thank you," she mumbled. *For nothing*, she thought to herself while hobbling out of the agency on her one good boot. Several people gawked as she walked past, but she ignored them.

Finally reaching her car, Lia rested her head on the steering wheel. Things had gone from bad to worse in a hurry. First, getting demoted from her job in the art department of a fashion magazine when they downsized their Savannah branch. Afterward, getting into an argument with the new boss she'd once been the superior of had dug her deeper into a hole.

Lia ended up fired, and without good references to find a new job. She did some freelance photography and graphic design on the side, which was enough to survive, but not for long. When her savings ran out, she'd have to ask her family for help, though she despised the thought with every fiber of her being. The disappointment in her father's eyes—the lectures about being responsible—the questions about why she had yet to have a family of her own when both her sisters had already settled down. It was too much to deal with at the moment.

Hearing a beep from her purse, Lia took out her cell and noticed her dad's number scroll across the screen. She had to tell him about her struggles sooner or later, but right now she'd rather be stung by a swarm of wasps than try to explain how she'd lost her job. Somehow, she'd kept it secret for an entire month by ignoring her father's calls. She wrote short vague texts to keep him happy and cooked up excuses for why she couldn't come over for visits. However, things were coming to a breaking point.

Lia took the long way home, debating what to do. When she entered her apartment, happy meows lifted her mood. "Hey Tatertot. I bet you're hungry, aren't you?" The yellow tiger-striped cat rubbed against her leg as Lia reached into the cabinet for a can of food. After putting the food in his dish, she sat on the floor next to him and stroked his back.

"What should we do, boy? Just when I think things can't get much worse, they do." Tatertot continued eating his food, content as always to have a full belly and be with his human. She sighed. "Sometimes I wish I could just be a cat. It must be nice not to have to worry about these things." Tatertot finished eating and crawled into her lap, kneading and purring like a lawnmower motor. "You wanna cuddle? Okay, that sounds like a plan."

Lia woke up on the couch in the evening with her phone buzzing like a beehive on steroids. This time it was her sister, Mia, and she'd left several messages.

"Lia, where have you been?" her older sister said when she answered.

"I'm sorry," she mumbled, trying to wake up. "Just busy."

"Dad has been trying to get ahold of you all day."

Lia pinched the bridge of her nose, blinking to clear her vision. "Why?"

Mia released a weary sigh. "Nana fell the other day. She's in the hospital in Savannah."

"She what?" Lia sat up, her heart drumming at the thought of her grandmother injured. "Is…is she all right?"

"She sprained her ankle. Besides that, and a couple of scrapes and bruises, she seems okay, but her doctor wants to keep her overnight for observation. I'll spend the night at the hospital with her tonight, but will have to go back to Atlanta tomorrow. Will you be able to help?"

"Yeah, of course. I'll be there first thing in the morning."

If only she'd picked up her phone yesterday instead of allowing her pride to get in the way. Lia peeked through the curtain, while trying to ignore the guilt coursing through her veins. When she saw her grandma sitting up in bed, smiling and talking with a female doctor, the knot in between her shoulder blades released.

"There you are, Lia," Nana said, noticing her right away. "Stop hiding behind that curtain and come talk to me."

She obeyed and walked in, attempting to push down a lump in her throat. "I'm sorry I didn't come yesterday."

"Oh, don't worry about clumsy ole me. I know you have your own life. Besides, I'll be out of here soon." Nana beckoned her forward. "Now come here and give me a hug." Lia did as she asked before sitting on the edge of the bed. "Dr. Fuller, this is my granddaughter, Natalia."

The doctor finished writing a few notes and smiled at her. "It's nice to meet you."

"You too. How is my grandmother doing?"

"She was a little dehydrated when she came in, so we've been giving her fluids and some antibiotics for a cut on her leg. If her blood tests come back normal, she should be able to go home with a boot for her ankle as early as tomorrow."

She breathed a sigh of relief. "Thank you."

"You're welcome. Will you be taking her home? She might need someone to help her for a few days."

"Yes, I'll go home with her," Natalia answered without even thinking. However, staying at her grandma's home on Sparrow Island sounded like a peaceful escape—the perfect place to think and contemplate how to improve her current situation.

"Oh, you don't have to do that," Nana protested. "I know you have your job at the magazine. I wouldn't want you getting fired because of me."

Lia bit her lip for a moment and shook her head. Now wasn't the time to reveal her job situation. Instead, she managed a smile. "Don't worry about that, Nana. They'll understand. Right now, you're my highest priority."

"Oh, thank you, dear. You're so sweet." She turned back to the doctor. "Isn't my Lia sweet? And so talented. Did I tell you she works for a big, fancy fashion magazine?"

The doctor shook her head, smiling. "No, you didn't, ma'am. I'm sure you're very proud of her."

"Yes, I am. She's going to accomplish big things. One day she'll be CEO, I'm sure of it."

Lia released a nervous laugh to mask her secret. "Oh Nana, stop bragging."

"Sorry, I get a bit carried away sometimes."

Lia composed herself and held her hand. "That's all right. I'm just glad to hear you're going to be fine."

She heard the curtain slide open, and Mia came in, frowning at Lia before turning her attention to the doctor. "How is my nana doing?"

The doctor explained a second time before leaving the room. Afterward, the tension in the room was enough to make anyone crazy. Finally, when Nana said she was going to take a nap, Mia asked her to go for a walk.

"Are you going to be able to handle things here, or should I stay longer?" Mia asked as they came out to the hallway.

Lia lifted her chin in a vain attempt to seem taller beside her sister. It was no use. She was at least five inches taller, beautiful, and perfect, even in her eighth month of pregnancy. She'd hardly gained any weight but sported a perfectly round beach ball-like baby bump. The perfection was almost too much, causing Lia to spout out a smart retort. "Well, I haven't had any mishaps so far, but give me a few minutes. I'm sure I could find some way to mess up."

Mia scoffed at her sarcasm. "I'm sorry. It's just, the past few days have been tough."

Lia sighed in resignation. "I understand. I shouldn't have been so short with you. Anyway, I've decided to stay with Nana for a week at least."

Mia's eyes widened. "Are you sure you can take that much time off? I'd hate for this to impact your career. I know how much you love your job."

Lia waved away her concern like a large fruit fly hovering around them. "I have vacation time," she lied. "Besides, you've done so much. Now it's my turn to help out." She stared into

Mia's eyes, mustering fake confidence. "I can do this, sis. Honest."

Mia paused before offering a slow nod. "All right. I trust you. But you have my number in case. Don't be afraid to call me any time."

Lia nodded. "Of course. Don't worry. Everything will be fine."

Her sister enveloped her in a tight hug as a foreboding feeling spread through Lia's heart. Had she just dug herself an even deeper grave? Could she really help her nana back on her feet when she couldn't even walk by herself without stumbling and fumbling everything up? Regardless, she was committed now.

2

*S*parrow Island. The name evoked a thousand childhood memories. They flowed through her brain like the evening tide—memories of picnics on the beach, searching for shells, and building sandcastles. She grinned, remembering the time her younger sister, Val, had her bag of chips stolen by a mischievous seagull. Her sister had chased the gull, screaming and waving her arms as if the bird would listen. "I hate birds!" she'd shouted afterwards, stomping back to the picnic blanket in a huff.

The ferry's horn drew Lia out of her daydream. "This is our stop," Nana announced.

Lia helped Nana get back into the car. It wasn't until they drove away from the ferry that she noticed something was off. "Nana, we're not on Sparrow. This island is way too large."

Her nana chuckled as Lia continued driving. "Didn't you listen to anything I told you while we were on the ferry? I'm having some construction done on my house. I'm living at an apartment here on Hopper temporarily."

Lia's mouth hinged open. "What?"

"Oh, it's no big deal. Since your grandpa passed away, the

house hasn't been kept up like it used to. The hurricane was the last straw. I hired a company to make repairs. They should be finished in a month."

Lia drew in an uneasy breath. "Oh...um that's okay," she managed but struggled to disguise the disappointment in her voice. To be honest, after the initial shock of Nana in the hospital, she'd been looking forward to staying at the old house. When Nana was sleeping or didn't need her for anything, it would have been relaxing to sit on the beach by herself and clear her thoughts, or since it was early spring, photographing the majestic purple petals of the magnolia tree in the garden would have been a fun pastime. Now, they were headed to some apartments she'd never heard of on Hooper Island.

While Lia tried to rein in her disappointment over their change in destination, Nana gave her directions to Hopper Ear Cove. Before too long, she'd parked in the lot behind one of the buildings. To her surprise, when they got out of the car, there was a young woman about her age waiting for them.

Nana recognized her right away and hobbled over to give her a hug. "Lia, this is Alicia. She and her husband are the new owners of the apartment complex. Alicia, this is my grand-daughter I told you about."

Alicia's blue-gray eyes twinkled in the afternoon sun. "Welcome, Lia! Your grandmother has told me so much about you. Here, let me help you carry things inside."

Lia thanked her and they made their way inside apartment sixteen. She scanned the room, noting the simple but adequate space and basic furniture. "How long have you lived here, Nana?" she asked while helping her grandma into a nearby recliner.

"About a month. Alicia and her husband Jace go to my church. When they found out about my house needing repairs, they told me about this vacant apartment. It was fully furnished, so I didn't have to worry about moving any big furniture in."

"That's nice." She turned to Alicia. "Thank you for helping Nana. It's a relief to know she has such good friends."

Alicia shrugged. "Oh, it was no problem at all. I lived here until last fall when Jace and I were married, and since there wasn't a big demand for the apartment, I left most of my furniture. When we heard Luna needed a furnished apartment, we were happy to help. God worked everything out seamlessly."

Lia nodded but didn't reply. While her nana had a strong faith, it was never something she'd gotten into herself. "Where do you and your husband live?"

"Apartment twenty, all the way at the end. It's a nice place for right now, but by next year we'll be moving to a house on the Hopper Ear Cove Lookout. Once we fix it up anyway. It's one of the oldest homes on the islands.

Lia smiled, knowing she would like Alicia. She was so nice and down to earth. "It sounds charming. I'd love to see it sometime."

"Sure! Just say the word and I'll give you a tour. Also, please let either Jace or me know if you need anything while you're here. We'd be happy to help in any way we can."

Lia bit her lip. "I had one more question. Do you allow pets? My neighbor is taking care of my cat right now, but it's only a temporary arrangement."

Alicia nodded. "Yes, we're pet friendly around here, as long as the tenants clean up after them. We do have a two-pet limit, but it sounds like that won't be an issue."

"Yep, it's just my Tatertot. He's a good boy."

Alicia giggled. "That's a fun name for a cat. You'll have to introduce me to him."

"Sure, I should have him by tomorrow."

Alicia let out a happy sigh. "Well, if the two of you will excuse me, I have to get back to the office."

They said their goodbyes, and after Alicia left, Lia sat on the

couch diagonal from her nana. "Well, home sweet home…
temporarily anyway. Alicia seems nice."

Nana nodded and reclined back. "Yes, she's made me feel
right at home. Her husband is nice too. He leads the contemporary worship service at the Merriweather church."

She lifted an eyebrow. "Oh really?"

"Yes, he's a very talented young man." Nana's eyes took on a
thoughtful gleam. "Would you believe only about six months
ago Jace had brain surgery to cure debilitating seizures?"

Lia shook her head with wide eyes. "Wow, so I'm assuming
the surgery worked?"

"Yes, so far he hasn't had any more seizures. He'd dealt with
them for many years, but then Alicia moved to the island. I
think her being here inspired him to seek treatment. I've always
believed God works in ways we can't understand. This is a
perfect example of that."

"That's an amazing story, Nana. I'm glad the doctors were
able to help him." Lia got up to stretch. "Are you hungry for
lunch?"

Nana nodded. "Yes, a little. There's some microwave mac
and cheese in the cabinet. Sorry, it was shopping week when I
had my fall."

Lia crossed to the kitchen. "That's okay. I love mac and
cheese. I'll go out for a few things later. Are there any stores on
the islands?"

"Yes, they are small, but they have the basics," Nana
answered from the living room. "If you want meat or fresh
produce, you'll have to go to the mainland."

Lia reached for the sealed cup of mac and cheese. "Okay, I'll
stop by the grocery store tomorrow when I go to Savannah to
pick up Tatertot."

"Thank you, dear. What would I do without you?"

Lia grinned, the tension from the mainland lifting away. "I
think the real question is, what would *I* do without *you*, Nana?"

The next day, Lia emerged through Nana's front door with a cat carrier in one hand and a bulging grocery bag in the other. She left the cat carrier by the door and made it halfway to the kitchen when the paper grocery bag split open like an overripe watermelon. Lia watched in dismay as the contents scattered all over the floor. A container of blueberries burst open when it hit the ground, sending little blue orbs rolling in every direction. Lia attempted to avoid them, but her feet inevitably left little splats of bluish purple everywhere she stepped.

"Oh, what else?" Lia grumbled while grabbing a nearby laundry basket to hold the groceries. She had about half the groceries gathered into the basket when Nana came hobbling in the living room to survey the chaos.

"Oh dear. What happened?"

Lia sighed in exasperation while haphazardly tossing a few lighter groceries into the basket. "Just me, Nana. You might as well call me Hurricane Natalia. No matter how hard I try, everything I touch ends in disaster."

"Oh nonsense. It can't be that bad. Besides, I like how you decorated the floor. It looks fun, like someone had a paintball war in here. Personally, I'm jealous. I love to play paintball."

Lia peeked up at her in bewilderment. "You've played paintball?"

"Oh, yes. I was in a league once. Didn't you know?" Nana's lips twitched to hold in her amusement. It was no use, and she had to cover her laugh. "I'm sorry. Sometimes you've just got to laugh at the mishaps, my dear. Taking yourself so seriously all the time is exhausting and just plain dull."

Giggles bubbled up Lia's throat and soon came bursting out of her mouth. She sat in the middle of the blueberry splatters and laughed with Nana, allowing her previous frustration to wash away. However, within a few seconds, her laughter gave way to tears. Like a dam breaking, Lia couldn't stop her sobs from flowing out.

She felt Nana's hand on her shoulder. "I knew something was bothering you. Come on, sit at the table with me and let's talk."

"But the groceries...and...and Tatertot," Lia protested.

"They can wait a few minutes," Nana insisted.

Within a few minutes, Lia had composed herself and sat across the table from Nana while wiping her face with a tissue. She told her everything. Being demoted and then getting fired and struggling to find a new job. "If I don't pay my rent soon, the landlord will kick me out. I don't know what to do. I've never felt more lost."

Nana's hand covered hers. "Did you enjoy working at the magazine?"

"Sort of," Lia sniffled. "It wasn't quite the dream job I imagined, but it paid the bills." She wiped at her nose with a tissue. "Mia never liked the idea of me quitting college to take that job. I know she'd just love to say 'I told you so' now. Then she'd tell Dad, too."

"Don't worry about her opinion right now, or your father's for that matter. What counts is yours. What career can you imagine yourself in?"

Lia shook her head. "To be honest, Nana. Right now, I have no clue. That sounds pretty pathetic right?"

Nana shook her head. "Not at all. I think what you're going through is an early life crisis."

She chuckled and wiped some tears off her cheeks. "I've heard of a mid-life crisis before, but never an early life crisis."

A grin spread across Nana's face. "That's probably because I made it up."

"Nana!" Lia chuckled. "You never stop surprising me."

"Well, that's not entirely true. I can't remember the real name for it...but that doesn't matter. Now, listen for a moment and I'll explain." Nana sipped from a cup of coffee and her expression turned serious. "I went through something similar when I was your age. Believe it or not, I majored in fine arts. I thought I wanted to sing and dance on Broadway."

"I never knew that. Nana, why didn't you mention it before?"

Nana shrugged. "Your mother never even knew. My life took a different path, after I realized the life of a performer wasn't for me. I dropped out of college and took a job waitressing. For a while my life seemed so confusing and without a real purpose. Then I met your grandpa." Nana paused with a nostalgic gleam in her eyes. "We were married within six months and started that little resort together in Savannah. Then when our kids were grown, we left the business to your uncle and moved to Sparrow Island to retire. It wasn't how I imagined my life would turn out, but we were happy."

Lia shook her head in amazement. "I remember all those church skits and choirs you helped with when I was young. You were always good at teaching the kids how to act on stage. This explains so much, and I never had a clue."

"I spent years wandering in circles, believing I'd failed. Then I realized God gave me these special gifts to serve Him, even if things didn't turn out like I expected. It was all in His plan."

Lia sighed. "Oh, Nana. I wish I had faith like you."

Nana patted her hand. "You can. Do you remember any lessons from church where you were baptized as a little girl?"

"Some." She sighed and stared at the table. Talking to her nana reminded her of simpler times when they all used to attend the same church together. Not that Lia was completely opposed to church. It was just something she stopped going to after her mother passed away. Her dad turned bitter against God, and Lia just followed his example and quit attending church, too.

"Do some praying," her nana continued. "I have a spare Bible if you don't have one. He'll guide you to the answers you seek.

In the meantime, I'll loan you two months' rent, so you don't have to worry about losing your apartment."

Lia's eyes widened. "Oh, Nana. I can't let you do that. If Mia found out, she'd never—"

Nana waved away her concern. "You let me worry about Mia. All she needs to know is you've decided to stay with me for a month to help me get back on my feet."

Lia sighed and looked away from Nana, ashamed of what her life had become. "When it's actually the other way around? Nana, I don't want to be a burden on you."

Her eyes softened as she touched Lia's cheek. "You could never be a burden. Trust me. It will be like a gift to have you stay with me. I miss you."

Lia's shoulders loosened as some of the weight rolled off them. "I miss you too. Thank you. You've no idea how much this means to me."

"You're welcome. You know I'd do anything for my grand-children." She hugged her, but Lia still couldn't seem to smile, worried what would happen if Mia found out her life was crumbling to the ground.

"Now, is there something else bothering you?" Nana asked.

Lia bit her lip, not sure how to respond without allowing all her anxiety to tumble out like a load of gravel. "I think I also just need some time alone," she admitted. "I need to clear my head from all these negative thoughts swimming in it. Would you mind?"

"Of course! I understand. Why don't you take a trip to Sparrow today? I need you to pick up a few of my things and check in with the repairs anyway. While you're there, take some time to sit on the beach in front of the house and think. I know going there always helps give me some perspective. I'll help Tatertot settle in while you're gone."

She forced a smile. Her nana always knew the right advice to give. "Thank you. I think I'll take you up on that. But first, I'll clean up the mess I made in the living room."

"I'll help."

Lia shook her head with a raised brow. "You're supposed to be resting."

"Oh, nonsense." Nana grinned with a determined look in her eyes. "I sprained my ankle. I'm not decrepit...yet anyway. I'll make you a deal. If you'll carry the basket in here, I'll put things in the top shelves of the pantry, and you can take care of the heavier items that go on the bottom."

"It's a deal."

3

*A*ll her childhood memories of summers on Sparrow took a nose dive when she pulled into the driveway of Nana's house. It was a wreck with patches of roof gone and dilapidated siding with moss growing on it. The crew her nana had hired were swarmed around the house like a colony of bees, repairing their hive. A few of them took notice of her, but she ignored their unwanted attention.

After finding the leader of the crew and proving who she was, Lia went inside and gathered a few things Nana had requested, including her sewing machine and fabric. While her foot healed, she needed something to occupy her time, and had even promised to teach Lia how to make some simple quilting projects that week.

After gathering everything and loading it into the trunk of her car, Lia took Nana's advice and headed down the short path from the house to the beach, taking her camera along. She took her time while walking down the path, snapping pictures along the way. Observing the blowing grasses and wildflowers along the sides of the path brought a small measure of peace to her soul. It was one thing that hadn't changed in her absence.

It reminded her of the walks they'd take down to the beach during childhood. Mia would always be up front, carrying the picnic basket. Her younger sister would be romping through the grass, chasing butterflies, and Lia would always stay next to Nana. They'd had so many meaningful conversations during their walks that she'd treasured.

Arriving at the beach, Lia snapped a few good shots before sitting in the sand. The waves rolled in and out, making a consistent rhythm. Her nana had always told her if she listened hard enough, she could hear the heartbeat of the ocean. Lia closed her eyes and sat in silence as more memories from childhood washed over her. If only she could go back there—back to simpler times when her life made sense.

God, are you listening? Nana says You always are. I need some direction...or maybe even an entire map because my life seems to be full of dead ends. Can You help?

Lia heard the waves growing louder and opened her eyes just in time to see a wave rushing toward her. The evening tide had started to come in. She scrambled to stand up so her camera wouldn't get wet, but not fast enough to avoid soaking the seat of her pants. "Guess that's a no," Lia grumbled while brushing wet sand from her capris.

She headed back up the path, her wet feet caked with sand. Some of the construction workers turned to gawk as she passed. Lia tilted her body in such a way to avoid showing the sea-soaked back of her pants.

She'd almost reached the car when one of the workers let out a whistle. Lia rolled her eyes while slipping behind the wheel and slamming the door shut. She packed up her camera while growling to herself. Men. All the ones she'd ever fallen for loved to flirt, but when it came time to commit, they sprinted away faster than a professional athlete competing in the Olympics.

The sun hovered lower on the horizon, and Lia didn't enjoy

traveling on the ferries after dark. She made it halfway to the ferry slip when something began squealing and knocking. "Just great," Lia muttered before she pulled over and checked under the hood. Billowing smoke poured out, and the smell of burnt rubber assaulted her nostrils. Coughing and hacking, she left the hood open to cool off and returned to the driver's seat. Her head rested against the steering wheel. Why had her high maintenance vehicle decided to develop a car flu today of all days?

After taking a few minutes to think, Lia reached for her cell to call Nana. "Oh, sorry honey," she finally answered after Lia redialed several times. "I was soaking in the tub. Is something wrong?"

Lia explained the situation and her location on Sparrow before a disconcerting beep interrupted. "Oh, my phone's going dead. Hold on a sec." She reached for her charging cable in vain. "Nana, is my phone charger there?"

There was a pause and the sound of her nana shuffling across the floor with her boot before she answered. "Yes, it's plugged in by the couch. Why?"

"It's my only one." Lia groaned while raking her fingers through her hair. "Well, I guess I can only talk to you until my battery dies."

"Just sit tight. I'll look through my phone book and…" Nana's voice faded out.

"Nana?" Lia said in desperation. "Are you there?" She pulled her phone away from her ear to look at it, but a lifeless blank screen stared back. Tossing her phone into the passenger seat, Lia fought back the urge to throw a childish temper tantrum at her misfortune. Instead, she got out of the car and closed the hood forcefully before pacing back and forth on the side of the road.

Who would hear or see her all the way out here? In the ten minutes since breaking down, she hadn't seen any traffic go by, and it was growing dark outside. Sparrow was the least populated island in the chain besides Skye. It was one of the reasons she escaped to her nana's house during summer breaks from school. She never dreamed her peaceful island refuge would become like Alcatraz, with the ocean imprisoning her on all sides.

As thirty minutes passed by, Lia sat in her car again and watched the last remnants of light sink beneath the horizon. She had two options—walking to the nearest house or spending the night in her car. Not wanting to look like a weirdo knocking on doors after nightfall, Lia opted for the latter and started rolling up her fleece jacket for a makeshift pillow. Maybe a night under the stars would help her gain perspective. Lia could only hope.

Zachery Nolan had just tucked his daughter in for bed when a familiar ringtone sounded from his pocket. He tried to answer his cell before it woke Violet, but her blue eyes popped open like it was Christmas morning. He silenced the phone and leaned over to kiss her forehead. "Everything's fine. Go back to sleep."

A pout formed on Violet's lips. "But you didn't finish the bedtime story."

He grinned and smoothed back her honey brown hair. "I tried, but you fell asleep. I'll read the ending again tomorrow night. Now, close your eyes. Colby will stay in here and protect you, won't you, boy?"

The massive Saint Bernard lifted his head from the rug across the room for a moment, before letting out a tired groan and collapsing back into a comfortable position on the floor.

Zach chuckled at the dog's weak vote of confidence and turned back to Violet. "I'll be downstairs making a phone call if you need me." He winked. "Still have Henrietta?"

"Yep." Violet grinned, pulling her stuffed animal chicken

from underneath the covers. She made the little hen bounce closer to him with adorable little clucking sounds.

"What is she telling me?"

"Henrietta says goodnight. She'll stay awake with me until I fall asleep."

Zach patted the stuffed animal's head. "Good chicken. I knew I could count on you. Goodnight Henrietta, and goodnight Violet."

Violet clucked for the chicken before covering a yawn. "Goodnight Daddy."

After she closed her eyes, Zach left the room, leaving the door cracked open a few inches before carefully navigating the stairs to the main level. He paused at the bottom to smile at a picture of his daughter as a toddler. When they'd moved to Sparrow Island, it had been one of the first portraits he'd hung on the wall. While he loved seeing her wispy pigtails and toothy grin, it also served as a stark reminder of how much Violet had grown in four short years. She had one year left before she'd start kindergarten—a thought that both excited and terrified him at the same time.

Zach shook the thought away and remembered the missed call on his cell. His neighbor, Luna Diaz, had left a voicemail. She was a sweet older lady from a few houses down who had occasionally watched Violet for him when he attended business meetings on the mainland. Since the hurricane damaged her house, she'd asked him to drive by her house occasionally to check on the repair crew's work. Zach didn't mind helping out. However, Mrs. Diaz never called after nine. Knowing it had to be urgent, he skipped listening to the voicemail and returned her call.

"Oh, thank goodness you called back!" Luna's anxious voice exclaimed after the first ring. "I'm sorry for disturbing your evening, but I've called about everyone I know on the islands without any luck. I hope I didn't wake Violet?"

Zach smiled and shook his head, although knowing Luna couldn't see him do so. "It's completely fine, Mrs. Diaz. How can I help you?"

"Oh, it's not for me." Luna paused and let out a weary sigh. "It's for my granddaughter. She was doing a favor for me, and her car broke down on Sparrow."

Zach agreed to help without delay after Mrs. Diaz explained the whole story. He'd met her granddaughter before the hurricane and remembered she'd had young children and was expecting another. A month or two had passed since then, and he guessed she had to be nearing her due date. The thought of a woman in her condition being stranded on the island bristled his conscious. There was no question. Of course, he would help.

It wasn't until after hanging up, Zach remembered Violet sleeping upstairs. He hated the thought of waking her up, but did he have a choice? Maybe a neighbor could come over to watch her. He scrolled through his phone contacts like a casino slot machine, hoping his finger would land on the name of someone who'd be willing to help instead of yelling at him for calling so late.

Zach stopped to rake his fingers through his hair. How did he get himself into these predicaments? His friends said he had a hero complex. He'd always denied it before, but now he wondered if it were true. Zach had agreed to help Luna's granddaughter without thinking of the needs of his daughter. However, he wasn't the type to go back on his word.

Zach looked at his phone again, but a voice stopped him from dialing.

"Daddy?" Violet called. "I still can't sleep."

A smile curved on his mouth when he saw the shadow of his daughter sitting on the top step with a larger shadow of Colby sitting beside her. "I can't sleep either. Want to go for a drive?"

4

*B*right lights awoke Lia from a restless sleep. She squinted, disoriented at first when she noticed her surroundings. It took a few seconds to remember she'd broken down on the road. Was it morning already? A glance out the window told her otherwise. It was pitch black outside, besides the two beams of light piercing through the back window.

Lia shielded her eyes while peering into the rear-view mirror. A man's shadow approached on the driver's side. Maybe a local police officer? She rolled down her window a few inches but kept up her guard. The residents on Sparrow were nice when she was a child, but who knew what kind of weirdos could have moved in since then? She gulped back her apprehension as the man stopped beside her and leaned toward the driver's-side window.

"Are you Luna Diaz's granddaughter?"

"Y-yes," she replied, observing the man didn't wear a uniform, but a fitted T-shirt instead, and he held a toolbox in one hand. "How did you know that?"

"I'm your grandma's neighbor, Zach Nolan. She called and said you were stranded here."

"Oh." Lia sighed and the knot between her shoulder blades released. "Thank you. My phone went dead, and I didn't think anyone was coming."

"You're welcome." He paused for a moment before tilting his head toward the front of her car. "Want to pop the hood so I can look for the problem?"

Lia blinked hard and nodded as her thoughts began to clear. "Of course." She pulled the lever and felt the click of the hood as it popped up. Zach thanked her and walked around to the front of the car. Feeling more comfortable around the stranger now, Lia unlocked the door and got out, joining him as he leaned over to inspect the engine. "How can I help?"

His eyes widened, as if seeing her for the first time. "I'm sorry. I thought I'd met you before at your grandmother's house. It was my mistake."

Lia chuckled, noticing he'd looked at her stomach first. "Oh, you probably thought I was Mia, right? She's my older sister, and about ready to pop."

"Okay, it's starting to make sense now. Thanks for clearing that up."

"No problem."

Zach continued to study her for a moment, before shaking his head as if in a trance. "If you could hold a flashlight, that would be great." She agreed, and he pulled one out of his toolbox for her. "Now, what did you notice before it broke down?"

Lia aimed the beam of light directly at the part of the engine he was looking at. "It made a squealing noise, and then a loud clunk. Smoke was everywhere."

Zach's brow furrowed at he listened. "Sounds like a transmission problem."

"Is that expensive to fix?"

"Maybe. I won't know until I take a closer look." Zach worked while he talked. She couldn't help being distracted by his buff arm muscles. He wasn't tall by any means—maybe a couple inches more than her five-four stature, but he made up for that with broad shoulders and a toned upper body. Lia had never been very attracted to men with facial hair, but his neatly kept moustache and beard suited him well. "How's your grandma doing?" he asked, drawing her attention back to his face. "I heard about her fall."

"Oh, Nana's doing as well as can be expected. The hardest part is convincing her to relax. She's stubborn and still insists on doing dishes and laundry even though I'm staying in her apartment to help with those things."

Zach chuckled, but still focused on the task at hand. "Sounds like Luna all right. But I'm sure she appreciates your company more than anything else."

"Yeah, you're probably right." Lia bit her lip as the sea breeze tousled the wispy hair around her face. "She's been asking me to come for a visit for months. I wish it hadn't taken her becoming injured to get my attention."

Zach's face took on a serious expression. "We all have busy lives. Sometimes all we can do is just try our best...um...what was your name? I don't think I asked before."

"Natalia Diaz."

He turned to grin at her. "Pretty name."

Lia's free hand rested on one hip, and she smiled. "It's a mouthful though."

"Can I call you Nat for short?"

She scrunched her nose. "My uncle calls me that, but I prefer Lia. Nat reminds me too much of those pesky fruit flies that show up around my kitchen sink."

He laughed again while loosening a bolt. "Well, since you definitely don't remind of one of *those* type of gnats, Lia it is."

"Thanks." Lia grinned, enjoying his subtle humor. Even when he didn't laugh, his mouth always seemed to be concealing something humorous he wouldn't speak out loud.

A few moments later, he sighed, and his happy expression faded. "Sorry. As I suspected, it looks like the transmission."

"Which means?" she asked, her hopes sinking.

"It's not something I can fix tonight." He wiped his hands on a rag and pulled out his cell. "It's almost eleven, so that means you'll miss the ferry even if I drive you."

Lia groaned and leaned against the car. "Well, thanks for trying to help. If you could just give me a ride back to my nana's house, I'd appreciate it."

Zach closed the hood and turned to her with an arched brow. "Are you sure?"

"I'll be fine. The house is a wreck, but Nana's furniture is still there. I'll sleep on the couch."

"The house isn't just a wreck. It's condemned. The roof could fall and crush you in the middle of the night."

Lia shrugged. "Well, I don't see any other option."

"I have a spare room with a futon."

Lia cringed and took a step back with her arms crossed. "Thanks, but I couldn't impose."

Zach offered a half grin. "I promise I don't have a criminal record, and I'm not a serial killer or anything like that."

A nervous chuckle escaped Lia's lips as she arched an eyebrow. "Sounds like something a serial killer would say."

He laughed before attempting an earnest expression. "Really, I wouldn't feel right leaving you in that old house, especially after promising Luna I'd look out for you. The spare bedroom is upstairs across from my daughter's room and the futon is comfortable."

Lia felt her walls of defense were crumbling like the graham cracker pie crust of her grandma's chocolate crème pie. It did sound better than staying in a house that looked more like a construction zone. She replayed his words in her mind, concentrating on one subtle comment he'd made. "Wait, you have a daughter?"

He nodded, his expression softening. "Yeah, Violet's four. She's sleeping in the backseat if you don't believe me."

Alarms went off in her head as she moved toward his SUV. "Your daughter is in the car? I wish you would have told me! I'd have told you to forget about the car for the night."

"She's fine. The air conditioner's going." He pulled a ring of keys out of his pocket. "I've got one of those cool key fobs that let you run everything from outside the car." He pushed a button, and the interior lights came on.

She peered through the back window, seeing a cute little girl with brown hair fast asleep in a safety seat, clutching tightly to a plushy chicken. Lia's heart melted and her resolve crumbled completely. Maybe Zach was a good guy after all. "All right," she said, looking over at him. "I'd appreciate a place to stay for the night."

Had his hero complex finally gone too far?

Zach filed through the possible repercussions of his decision while pulling into the driveway. Sure, Lia was Luna's granddaughter, but that didn't guarantee she was trustworthy. To top it off, he'd offered the guest room right across from where his daughter slept? In normal circumstances he would have offered to drop her off at a hotel, but the secluded nature of the island made that impossible. Zach remembered the brave and determined look in her eyes when she insisted on staying in her nana's broken-down house. However, his conscience wouldn't allow him to even consider that. Luna trusted Zach to help her granddaughter, and he considered himself responsible for her safety now—at least for the night.

Zach parked the car and turned to Lia, who'd been hugging her purse with a vice grip the entire drive. "Well, this is home sweet home. Doesn't look like much from the outside, but I hope you'll be comfortable."

Lia's eyes scanned his property, illuminated by a row of solar lights, trailing up the walk to the front door. "Thank you, Zach. It will do just fine, and I appreciate your kindness."

"It's no problem, and please feel free to make calls from the house phone. I'm sure your nana is concerned about you." He stepped out and opened the back door to get Violet out of her booster seat. Once he had her in his arms, Zach led the way up the path toward the house. After they were inside, he showed Lia the phone in the kitchen and excused himself to put his daughter in the master bedroom for the night. A cuddler by nature, she usually sleepwalked there at some point during the night anyway.

When he returned, Lia had just hung up the phone. She covered a yawn before offering him a shy smile. "Nana said to thank you again for helping me."

"No problem. Do you think she'll be all right without you there?"

Lia sighed while relaxing onto a stool at the breakfast bar. "I think so. Nana's been up and around faster than her doctors expected. She's one feisty woman."

Zach nodded with a chuckle. "Yeah, Luna is one of a kind."

They studied each other for a few moments before Lia broke the silence. "Well, your daughter is a good sleeper, isn't she? She didn't stir once in the car or when you brought her inside."

"Yep, once she falls asleep, she's usually out for the night. It's the convincing her to go to sleep part that's the most difficult."

"High spirited?"

"You can say that again."

Lia giggled and yawned again. "So was I."

"Well, I'll show you the guest room upstairs so you can get some rest. I also have an extra phone charger you can use up there for your phone." She agreed and Zach led her upstairs.

"Thanks, I'm exhausted." Her drowsy smile made his heart pound. Even in the darkness, he'd noticed her beauty, but the light enhanced her bright hazel eyes and long raven hair. He wanted to talk with her more, but that would have to wait until morning.

$\mathcal{W}$hat was that sound? It was a high pitched and bird-like screech she couldn't place.

Lia drifted to consciousness and as soft light filtered through the sheer curtains, yesterday's events came flooding back to her. After Lia's car broke down, Nana's neighbor had come to the rescue and offered her a place to stay for the night.

She blinked several times before reaching for her phone on the nightstand to see the time. It was half-past six. In spite of only getting less sleep than usual, she felt rejuvenated. Sleeping on the couch for a few nights at her nana's, she'd developed a sore neck, but this morning the problem had resolved. Maybe sleeping on a futon had helped. She texted her grandma to check in and was relieved to find out Nana was doing fine and Tatertot was adjusting to his new living situation.

After setting her phone aside, a strange screeching sound filtered into the room again. This time Lia recognized the noise as a rooster's crow. A bleating of a goat followed, and last, a honking goose. What in the world? Was this some crazy Wizard of Oz dream, except in reverse? Dorothy had fallen asleep in

Kansas and woken up in Oz, but maybe Lia had been transported from Sparrow Island to Auntie Em's farmhouse instead?

Lia crossed to the window while rubbing the sleep out of her eyes. Opening the blinds confirmed it hadn't been a dream after all. Zachery Nolan's spacious backyard was a menagerie of little sheds with animals going in and out. Along the border of the yard, some animals were in enclosures separated by fences, but in the center, there was a garden and a pond. The smaller animals, like the chickens, ducks, and geese, were allowed to wander freely in that area. Lia had never seen anything like it.

Mind still reeling, Lia glanced into a small mirror over the dresser to fix her hair and wipe away a smear of mascara under one eye. The smell of cooking food lured her out of the room and down the stairs to a spacious kitchen. The huge St. Bernard she'd met last night greeted her first. Lia patted Colby's head while observing her surroundings. Zach had his back turned away from her, flipping pancakes on an electric griddle, and there were sausage patties and eggs sizzling in pans on the stove.

His daughter sat on a stool pulled up to the marble topped breakfast bar. The little girl's sapphire eyes lit up when she saw her. "Daddy, she's awake!"

"Morning," she murmured with a shy wave and took a step back. Hopefully her breath didn't smell too bad that morning.

Zach turned away from the pancakes for a moment and grinned at her. "Good morning. After yesterday's ordeal, I didn't expect you up so early."

"I...I'm an early riser anyway." She turned to look outside as a black chicken with white stripes pecked at the sliding glass door, providing a welcome distraction from Zach's sky-blue eyes. It had been too dark last night to notice them, but now they threatened to reel her in.

"I'm Violet," the little girl piped up.

Lia turned her attention to Zach's daughter, relieved to

31

notice he was flipping pancakes again. "It's nice to meet you. I'm Lia," she offered with a smile. "Is that your chicken outside?"

Violet nodded. "That's Cookie."

"That's a nice name. Did you pick it out?"

"Yep!" Violet said as a radiant smile bloomed on her lips. "I've named all our chickens." Her smile faded for a moment. "I also named Henrietta, but she died."

"I'm sorry to hear that. I'm sure you miss Henrietta a lot."

Violet nodded with a sniffle. "She was old, but I have a pretend Henrietta now." She pulled out a red plushy chicken she'd been holding onto last night.

"Violet was so heartbroken when Henrietta died, Luna made that plushy for her last year," Zach added while he continued to work on breakfast. "It helped Violet feel better."

Lia's heart warmed, and she looked at the plushy with new eyes. "She never told me about that. How sweet."

He nodded in agreement. "Yeah, she's a blessing."

"Luna's our neighbor," Violet added, peering up at Lia with wide, curious eyes. "Do you know her?"

Lia nodded and sat on the stool next to Violet. "Yes, I do. Actually, Luna is my Nana."

The little girl tilted her head like a beagle puppy Lia had when she was a child. "Do you mean a nanny? I had one of those one time."

Lia shook her head, offering Violet a kind smile. "No, a nana. That's another name for grandma."

"Oh," Violet said as her eyes filled with understanding. "I had a grandma too, but daddy said she went to heaven before I was born."

"I'm sorry. Well, at least you'll meet her there one day. I bet she'll be so excited and give you a big hug."

Violet grinned and hugged her chicken closer. "That's what Daddy always says."

Lia smiled as she met Zach's eyes and a wave of ease flowed

through her. How had she come across such an adorable little family so unexpectedly? He turned back to the stove as the sausage sizzled, prompting Lia to approach. "How can I help?"

"You're our guest. You don't need to do anything."

Lia braced her hands on her hips. "I'm not some damsel in distress who needs to be waited on." She motioned toward the carton of eggs. "I can scramble those if you want."

Zach sighed and raised an amused brow. "Sure, that would be nice. I guess I do have my hands full with the pancakes and sausage."

"Yeah, I can see that." Lia chuckled before she opened the egg carton and stared at it for a few moments. They were all different sizes and colors, ranging from white, shades of brown, and even a few green and blue. She picked one up that looked like an oversized robin egg to study it. "Are you sure these are safe to cook?"

Zach laughed again. "Yeah, that one's from one of our Americauna chickens. I promise you they're just like other eggs and fine to eat."

Lia shrugged and busied herself cracking the unusual eggs into a bowl. Just like Zach said, the yolks were all the same. She whipped them up with a nearby fork and poured the scrambled mixture into a heated pan coated with olive oil.

"I'm having your car towed back here, if that's all right," Zach said while turning a sausage patty over with a spatula. "I think I can save you some money if I pick up the replacement part and install it myself."

"You don't have to do that. I'm sure you have enough on your plate...raising Violet, and I'm sure you have to go to work at some point."

"It's no problem. Really. I work from home, so I make my own schedule."

Lia concentrated on the eggs as they sizzled and fluffed up in the pan. "That's interesting. What do you do?"

"Web design. What about you?"

"Well, that's…complicated at the moment." She chopped at the eggs harder than necessary, remembering the smug look on her former boss Marcela's face when she fired her. "You might say I'm in the process of a career change. I'm looking for a temporary part time job here on the islands."

"Nothing wrong with that. You'll find a better job soon. I went through something similar about four years ago. Now I love my job, and since I'm home, I get to spend more time with Violet."

"I'm happy to hear that," Lia responded while continuing to fume on the inside. She felt Zach's eyes watching her, but tried to ignore it.

"Forgive me for asking this…but are you all right? Is it something I said?"

"What do you mean?" She noticed him glancing at the pan and she gasped, realizing the eggs had been chopped and pounded into submission until they were mush. Lia sighed and covered her face. "Oh my…sorry for punishing the eggs."

He chuckled softly and reached for the spatula. "It's all right. We have plenty of eggs. I'll just save these to give the animals later. They love table scraps. Why don't you put the plate of pancakes and sausage on the table while I work on a second batch of eggs."

Lia did as he asked, grateful to be out of the spotlight. Why did the whole job situation with her former boss bother her so much? Honestly, she had hated her job, with all the petty people and drama. It took her a while to realize it was all a big trap. Her career at the magazine had been like stepping into quicksand. She reasoned if she paid her dues, eventually there'd be a promotion toward her dream job. Instead, she'd been sucked in deeper and deeper, until she didn't know how to escape.

By the time Zach finished the second round of scrambled eggs and sat them on the breakfast bar, Lia had calmed down.

However, as they ate, some of her anxiety came crashing back down on her. This time it wasn't about her lost job, but how she'd destroyed the first batch of eggs. Zach had witnessed her odd behavior. Did he regret his good deed now and wonder what kind of weirdo he'd invited into his home for the night?

While Lia fretted and robotically consumed her meal, barely tasting it, Violet babbled on and on in the background like a little parrot. She talked about chickens and starting pre-school in the fall. Lia caught little pieces of the conversation, but most of all she was just relieved to escape the spotlight.

"Well," Zach said after they finished eating, "I guess it's about time to drive you back to Hopper."

Lia sighed in relief and stood up. "Yeah, I hate to eat and run, but I'm anxious to see Nana. She sounded all right on the phone, but I don't want her to do too much."

He nodded. "Of course. I completely understand."

Violet's lips formed a pout. "Do you have to leave already, Lia? I wanted to show you my chickens."

The little girl's pleading blue eyes reeled Lia in like a fish on a hook. "I guess I can stay for a few more minutes."

6

*C*olby led the way outside with a happy wagging tail, and Lia followed with a false sense of security. It wasn't until she reached the middle of Zach's backyard that she remembered her fear of birds. The chickens, who'd been peacefully nibbling on grass and garden plants had surrounded her. She squealed and hid behind Zach for protection as a few of the chickens rushed toward her and eyed the red polish on her toenails.

"It's all right," Zach said, chuckling as he shooed the stubborn chickens away. "They're harmless."

"Harmless? That's easy for you to say! Those tiny feathered dinosaurs weren't looking at your toes like they were delicious candy apples!" She clutched the back of his shirt, hiding her face against him.

A laugh rumbled through him. "I'm sorry. They are a little too curious sometimes."

Lia peeked through one eyelid. "Are they gone?"

"Yeah, Violet gave them the leftovers from breakfast."

She opened both of her eyes. Her fingers still clung tightly to Zach's shirt and Lia stepped back as warmth tingled through her cheeks. Sure enough, the chickens had refocused their attention to devour a few pancakes scattered on the ground.

Violet giggled while picking up the black and white chicken who'd been pecking at the door a few minutes before. "This is Cookie," the little girl said while coming toward her. "Want to pet her?"

Lia backed away with her hands up as a shield. "Not right now, sweetheart. I'd rather look at her from a distance."

"Pleeeeese?" Violet pleaded with puppy dog eyes. "She's our sweetest hen, and her feathers are sooo soft."

"She is really docile," Zach agreed. "But you don't have to if it makes you uncomfortable."

Lia gulped down a lump in her throat as the little girl continued to plead with her eyes. She'd have to put her childhood fear of birds aside. After all, what example was she setting for Violet if she was afraid to touch a little chicken? "Okay," she finally said and leaned closer to Violet and her terrifying feathered friend. Lia's fingers trembled as she reached toward the animal. When it made a low clucking sound, she recoiled.

"She's just saying hi," Violet reassured. "Cookie talks to me like that all the time."

"Okay," Lia said and tried again. *Don't be a coward. It's friendly. It's a friendly feathered dinosaur.* The thought almost made her giggle, recalling an article she'd once read about chickens being the closest remaining relative to dinosaurs. She didn't know if it had any truth to it, but Lia saw a resemblance. Finally brushing her fingers over the bird's feathers, a smile crept across her lips. "Wow, her feathers are like silk."

Violet's face lit up. "I told you!"

Lia petted the chicken a few more times and her shoulders relaxed. "You're actually really sweet, aren't you?" The curious little hen turned her head one way and then the other way to study Lia. "You're not scary after all. At least when you aren't goggling at my toes."

"Sorry, I probably should have warned you about that," Zach said from beside her. "I always wear work boots when I come out to tend to the animals, so I just didn't think about it. Chickens are attracted to colorful things, and red is their favorite color to peck at."

"So, my red toenails look like a chicken buffet?"

He nodded with a chuckle. "Basically...yeah. They should be occupied with eating the table scraps for a while though." He motioned out of the garden. "Do you want to see the rest of the animals? We have rabbits, a few pigmy goats, and even a potbellied pig."

Lia nodded, braver than before. "I'd love that."

She listened quietly as Zach introduced her to all the animals. Her favorites were the bunnies. There was one enclosure with a mother named Penelope who had a litter of tiny babies. Then they saw the goats, who were a little noisy for her liking, and last, a blind potbellied pig named George. "You have quite the collection of animals," she commented as Zach fed George an apple. "How did you find them all?"

He grinned while leaning against the fence. "We rescue animals from different places. Most of them have been abandoned or have conditions that would keep them from surviving on a farm. Some of the chickens were from the feed store. We buy the ones who were born with splayed legs or crooked toes...basically the ones other people look over."

She furrowed her brow. "Splayed leg?"

"Oh, sorry for not explaining. It's when their legs are bowed out and they can't walk. I have a little trick I used to help straighten their legs out. You'd never be able to tell their legs had ever been deformed."

"Wow, so you're kind of a chicken whisperer, huh?"

He rubbed his forehead. "Oh, I don't know about that. I've just watched a lot of videos online for how to help them. I don't like to see little creatures suffer. They wouldn't have survived without help."

"Well, I think what you're doing is awesome."

"Thanks. It's hard to believe we started out with some battery hens from an egg factory. My friend rescued some, but he couldn't keep all of them. So, we took six. The poor girls barely had any feathers and probably hadn't seen a blade of grass in their lives. Henrietta was one of them. She was the sweetest girl we've ever had."

Lia turned her attention to Violet who was over by the fence feeding some geese blades of grass. Colby stayed close to the little girl and sprawled out in the grass next to her. It was a sweet sight how the dog was so protective over her.

She turned back to Zach with a frown. "I'm sorry that you lost Henrietta. I can tell Violet misses her."

Zach nodded. "Thanks. It's hard when they pass on, but at least we know we gave her a happy life. It's a good experience for Violet, too. All of us experience loss at some point in our lives and have to learn to cope in a healthy way. Raising and helping animals will do that."

"I agree." She turned to study him as the morning sun highlighted his blue eyes. Men rarely surprised her, but Zach was the exception. How did he manage to have more depth than all the guys she'd dated combined?

He smiled at her. "Well, I guess we better head on over to Hopper now. I'd hate to keep your grandmother waiting."

Lia nodded while trying to ignore her pounding heart. "Thanks for everything, Zach."

"It's no problem." He opened the gate for her, and they made their way back into the garden. They were halfway back to the house when he turned and rubbed his chin. "Would you and your nana like to come over for an early dinner on Sunday? Violet has been missing her like crazy since she had to move to Hopper."

Lia managed a nod. She actually liked the idea of seeing Zach and his daughter again.

"Oh, by the way, the part for your car should come in on Monday if the Lord wills it. Then I can get started on fixing it for you."

"Thank you." She paused for a moment, hearing him mention God. He used the phrase so naturally, like her nana did. Why did that fact intrigue her so much? Whatever it was, she had three days to sort through her feelings or maybe less if her nana decided to play twenty questions when Zach drove her home.

During lunch, Lia took a sip of her iced tea and studied Nana with probing eyes. Twenty questions would have been better than no questions at all. Finally, she couldn't take the suspense any longer and put her cup back on the placemat. "Well, are you going to ask me or not? I'd rather talk about it now instead of being surprised by it later."

Nana looked up from her salad with an innocent smirk on her face. "Talk about what?"

Lia scoffed. "You know exactly what."

"Now you're talking in riddles, Lia."

"Zachery Nolan? You know, your neighbor?"

Nana's brown eyes lit up. "Oh, you want to talk about Zach? He's such a nice young man, isn't he? And his daughter is a sweetheart."

Lia slumped in her chair with a groan, exhausted from talking in circles. "Yes, they're very nice."

"Oh, please don't slouch. Your back will thank you for good posture in the future." Nana smiled as she stood from the table and began clearing the dishes.

Taking Nana's advice, Lia straightened in her seat. "I can wash the dishes. You should go in the living room and rest."

Nana lifted her chin in defiance as she crossed to the sink, hobbling on her booted leg. "Nonsense. The Bible speaks against having idle hands, and I've lived by those words my whole life. I'll probably never run a marathon at my age, but my hands are still well equipped for any task the good Lord gives me."

Lia sighed while crossing the room to grab a hand towel. "All right. Let's compromise. You can wash and I'll dry."

"Sounds good to me." Nana offered a playful wink. "We'll have plenty of time to talk about Zach and his daughter while we work. He's such a nice young man."

Lia rolled her eyes, realizing the conversation was inevitable. There was no point fighting against it. Somehow Nana coaxed people into talking about subjects they didn't want to, all the while making it seem like they came up with it first. There was no doubt in her mind, Nana was meant to be a telemarketer.

7

*R*unning a vet clinic on a secluded island, Kendall Mulligan's days were as unpredictable as waves on the shore. Some days customers would calmly filter through, and on others they would rage in like a storm surge. Now it was even worse with the influx of displaced animals after Hurricane Arley. She loved helping owners reunite with their pets, but the added responsibility was also taxing on her nerves.

During a break in the madness one Friday afternoon, Kendall tapped her fingers on the mobile desk while waiting for the new vet website to load. When an error message came up for the third time in a row, she closed her laptop with a frustrated sigh.

"Technology giving you trouble again?"

Kendall nodded as her assistant, Alicia came down the narrow hallway, cuddling a homesick kitten. "Always. You know, I thought I'd be saving money by setting up this website on my own, but it's constantly glitching! People have been calling in to tell me the new appointment calendar isn't working. I'm afraid this is going to make us lose customers."

Alicia moved closer. "Sorry. Want me to take a look at it? I don't know much about websites, but I could at least try. Maybe you could take Zoe out for a walk and get some fresh air while I do."

Kendall's Australian Shepherd's ears perked up, and the dog sat at her feet with a happy panting tongue. She smiled at Zoe and patted her furry head. "That sounds like fun, doesn't it, girl?" She looked back up at Alicia with a relieved smile. "Thank you for offering. I think some fresh air sounds wonderful."

Walking through the small town on Sparrow toward the ferry slip a few minutes later, Kendall was glad she'd accepted Alicia's offer. Driving to different islands in the chain made her days interesting with new scenery. Today they were parked on Sparrow. The beaches were perfect for a day of relaxation and in the distance, she spotted sailboats enjoying the beautiful afternoon calm. The island was also a popular place for surfers to come enjoy the waves.

Kendall breathed in the fresh salty air, relieved to be outside. She loved her new job, but sometimes being in the RV made her claustrophobic, especially on busy days like this. It had been wrong to assume working on the Independence Islands would be less stressful than the city.

After sitting on a shaded bench facing the sea, Kendall checked the email on her phone. When only junk mail popped up on the screen, she sighed. "Where are you, Tyler?" she whispered into the breeze. She scrolled through her messages, trying to find his last email. Had it been nine days since she'd heard from him? No, ten. Her finger tapped the message that confirmed it. He'd said then his squadron was on the move, and he might be hard to contact for a few days. He could never tell her exactly where he was, but maybe that was good. Less information would cause less fretting on her part.

They communicated through written letters often, even though it took an eternity to arrive, and others teased it was old-fashioned. To Kendall, it was a comfort holding a paper

Tyler had written by hand. However, she'd been spoiled by hearing from him at least once a week through email. Once in a while, they even used video chat, but what did this delay mean? It was probably nothing, but worry still coiled around her heart like a boa constrictor, squeezing tighter with each passing day. She watched the news at night, praying there wouldn't be a story about American soldier casualties overseas.

Zoe tugged on her leash, dragging Kendall's thoughts back to the present. She smiled down at her faithful companion. "All right, Zoe. I guess we should head back now."

Zoe led the way back to the RV, happily wagging her tail while Kendall became absorbed in her thoughts of Tyler again, but this time she knew what she needed to do—pray. There was no sense in worrying about what could happen. It wouldn't help Tyler or herself. *God, please protect Tyler. I'm placing him in Your hands because I know you love him even more than I do. Help me to trust You and thank You for your abundant blessings. I know You hear me. I know You have great plans for me and my loved ones. Thank You for showing me Your love in the everyday little things.*

By the time she ended the prayer, they were back to the RV, and a client had parked his car next to it. When the man got out with his daughter and huge St. Bernard, Kendall recognized him right away and smiled. "Hi, Mr. Nolan."

"Hi, Dr. Mulligan. Please feel free to call me Zach."

"Okay, Zach it is. I didn't expect to see you here for a while since Colby just had his yearly checkup. Is something wrong?"

He smiled at her while patting Colby's head. "Well, I was hoping you could tell me. I played fetch with Colby this morning and all of a sudden, he developed a limp. I hoped it would go away if he rested, but he seems so uncomfortable. I thought bringing him in was a good idea."

Kendall nodded while leaning down to pet Colby. "Well, I'm glad you did. It's better to be safe than sorry. Here, let's go inside and I'll take a look." Kendall opened the door and allowed Zach to go in first.

They barely made it up the first step when Colby faltered and released a high-pitched yelp as one of his front legs gave out. "Sorry, old buddy. I should have known better," Zach said and carefully lifted the mountainous dog in his arms. Kendall stood watching for a moment, in awe that Zach could lift a 150-pound dog with ease, before following behind him.

Alicia greeted them warmly before turning to Zach's daughter, Violet. "Hey sweetie. It's nice to see you again so soon. Want to pick out a piece of candy while Dr. Mulligan helps Colby?"

The little girl's eyes lit up like the fireworks on the Fourth of July. "Do you have Sweet Tarts?"

"I think so." Alicia reached for the candy bucket they kept stashed away in a cabinet in case any kids came into the clinic.

Meanwhile, Kendall followed Zach into the exam room. "If you could just put Colby right on the exam table, that would be great."

Zach did as she asked and stood by the table afterwards to keep the St. Bernard still. "I'm so grateful your mobile clinic was parked here on Sparrow today. I never would have thought he'd get injured just from a game of fetch."

Kendall nodded as she examined Colby's injured leg. "He's a senior dog, so it's not uncommon for him to start having some joint problems." She frowned while feeling an abnormality in his elbow joint. "I'm going to say it's most likely elbow dysplasia, but he'll have to have an x-ray to be sure."

Zach rubbed his forehead. "Will I have to go to the mainland for that?"

Kendall smiled with a shake of her head. "Nope, I've got one right here actually." She crossed the room and wheeled the mobile x-ray machine out of a storage cabinet. A sudden wave of loneliness crashed over her, remembering the day Tyler had helped install it when she first came to the islands. She said another silent prayer for his safety.

"Do you want me to carry Colby over there now?"

Kendall composed herself and returned her attention to Zach and his dog. "Yes, please. This shouldn't take long either."

After the x-ray was done, she looked at the film and confirmed her diagnoses. "We'll start with shots and a leg brace first. I'm hoping that will help with the pain and help it heal. The brace won't be in for about a week though. Until then, I'd recommend trying to keep him from too much activity."

Zach chuckled. "That will be easier said than done, but I'll try my best. Colby may be a senior, but he's got the heart of a pup. Isn't that right, boy?" Colby wagged his tail in response.

When the shots were done, Kendall led Zach and his St. Bernard back to the front of the RV where Violet sat eating her candy while petting Zoe with her free hand. Alicia sat at the front desk telling the little girl about her husband's service dog, Cooper. When Alicia finished, Kendall turned to her. "Could you set an appointment for Colby in about a week's time for a follow up and brace fitting please?"

"Sure thing," Alicia said and started opening up the spread-sheet. "Okay…um, wow, we're pretty booked up for next week, but we can fit you in next Friday around noon. Will that work?"

"Yep, that'll work fine." Zach glanced at the screen and let out a playful whistle. "Wow, you girls are busy! Do you even have time to eat lunch?"

Kendall let out a sardonic laugh. "We trade off most of the time, but it's still been kind of hectic lately. Especially while trying to work out the bugs on our new website. I think what we really need is a part-time secretary to help keep schedules straight."

Zach rubbed his chin. "I'd be happy to help with the website for free."

She smiled, feeling a huge weight lifting off her shoulders. "Oh, we would appreciate that, but we'll pay you of course."

He shook his head. "No, I couldn't charge you...not after all you've done for Colby. How about you come by tomorrow afternoon after your vet calls, and I'll take a look at it?"

"That sounds perfect."

"Good." He paused, looking deep in thought before speaking again. "You know...I think I might have a lead on a part-time secretary, too. She's new to the islands, but I'll see if she might be interested and let you know."

Nana pulled a completed quilt block from underneath the foot of her sewing machine. "It's so nice to be quilting again."

Lia smiled while petting Tatertot in her lap. "I'm glad."

She started piecing together a few more squares of fabric. "Maybe next, I could teach you how to make your own quilt. There's this adorable little quilt shop in Savannah I'd love to take you to sometime."

"I'd love that. Maybe we could go after your next doctor's appointment."

Nana nodded as she fed fabric through the sewing machine. "Sounds like a good plan." A moment later, it made a weird sound, and she stopped sewing. "The thread ran out. Guess I'll have to finish this later."

Lia frowned. "I'm sorry. You don't have any more in your sewing bag?"

Nana shook her head. "Not in this color. I do have a spool holder with my stash of threads hanging on the back of my closet door. I forgot to ask you to grab that for me."

"We could take your car and go get them if you want."

Nana waved away her suggestion. "Oh, I'd hate to ask you to

drive over there again. Especially after what happened with your car."

"Don't worry about that. It was a ticking time bomb and could have broken down any time. Besides, it will be lunch time by the time we come back. We could pick up something from the food truck I've seen stopping around the islands. Comfort Cuisine? I think that's what it's called. Anyway, I've heard the food is awesome."

"All right. I guess it would be nice to get out of the apartment for a little while."

Almost an hour later, they were loading Nana's trunk with her thread spools and a few other bags of miscellaneous stuff she'd brought back to the apartment. After helping her nana into the passenger side door and shutting it, Lia's eyes drifted toward Zach's house. There was a car parked in the driveway and he stood on the porch talking with someone she didn't recognize. While she was still looking, Zach turned and waved at her. Lia's heart jittered as she gave a slight wave back and escaped around to the driver's-side door. She slipped inside and buckled her seatbelt, attempting to ignore the heat tingling through her cheeks.

She felt Nana's eyes on her as she put the car into reverse. "Did you want to stop by Zach's house and check on your car?"

"Um...no, he has company. We'll see him tomorrow." She forced the words out quickly, praying her nana wouldn't say anything else. As Lia left, she stole a quick glance in the direction of Zach's porch. His guest was still there—a beautiful woman with curly auburn hair. They looked happy. Was she a girlfriend? It wouldn't surprise Lia. Most nice men like him were already attached. But why should she care anyway? That was a question with no easy answer.

8

*V*arious ingredients were scattered across the kitchen island as Zach leaned over the recipe book one more time to check how much flour he needed. After church, he'd rushed home to start on the homemade pizza dough. It was his mother's recipe, and it took a few hours to rise properly. He had a small window to ensure it would be ready by the time their guests arrived.

Violet came into the kitchen, still in her Sunday dress. She tugged on the bottom hem of his t-shirt. "Can I help, Daddy?"

He knelt to eye level with her and smiled. "You sure can, pumpkin. How about you change into your play clothes first though?"

"Okay!"

Zach stood again and started measuring out all the ingredients they'd need. He'd learned from experience that it was much easier to cook with a five-year-old when everything was prepared ahead of time. Her attention span shifted like leaves in the breeze sometimes. When she returned, he let her pour the ingredients into a large ceramic bowl on the counter. "Now be careful with the…" he said as she dumped the flour in all at once. "Flour," he finished as a powdery cloud mushroomed into the air.

Violet peeked at him with a sheepish grin, her face covered with a thin layer of fine powder. "Sorry Daddy."

"It's all right. Just be careful."

Everything else went in without a hitch, and before long it was time to knead the dough. Violet watched him intently. "You're really good at making dough."

"Thank you. Your grandma taught me how to do this when I was a kid."

"Grandma did?"

The girl's confused expression prompted him to explain. "Grandma was my mom. She taught me all kinds of things, like I'm teaching you."

"Oh," Violet replied, looking deep in thought. "Why don't I have a mommy?"

Zach paused with his hands on the dough for a moment. Violet had been asking more questions lately. She had an inquisitive mind, and he wondered how deep the questions would go this time. Finished kneading, Zach put the first ball of dough in a bowl and bent to Violet's level again. "We talked about this before, remember? You had a mommy. She was a wonderful person, but she was sick and didn't feel like she could take care of you."

"So, she brought me to you?" Violet asked.

He nodded. "Yep, that's right. That's when I became your daddy."

"Will Mommy ever come back?"

Zach gave her a knowing smile. He wondered and sometimes feared the answer to that question. "I don't know, pumpkin. I wish I did. But at least we have each other, right?"

Violet nodded, and her expression brightened. "And Colby."

He chuckled. "Yes, of course, Colby."

"And the chickens...and goats and rabbits?"

"Yep, them too. We're all a big happy family."

Violet started listing off all the other rescued animals in their backyard as Zach opened the plastic flour container again to sprinkle on the counter for the second ball of dough. He sighed while starting to knead it, relieved Violet was satisfied with his answers to her questions—at least for the time being. The identity of her mother was an inevitable question he'd have to answer someday, but he hoped to delay it until she was older. He didn't want Violet growing up feeling like an outcast like his sister had. She'd have a normal and happy childhood if Zach had anything to say about it.

Violet's innocent voice filtered through his thoughts. "You know what, Daddy?"

"What?"

"I like Lia. She's nice."

He nodded but kept his focus on the dough. "Yeah, you're right. She is. Are you excited about seeing her this afternoon?" The dough was a little sticky, so Zach reached for the container of flour.

"Yes! Maybe when she comes, I can ask her to be my new mommy!"

Zach fumbled with the container, and it plopped onto its side, sending flour cascading off the edge of the counter. He scrambled to right the container before it dumped completely out but only managed to save a little bit. When Zach looked down, he suppressed a laugh. His daughter's hair and shoulders were coated in fine, white powder and more flour rested in a pile at her feet. "Oh, Violet, I'm so sorry!"

Violet blinked a few times and rubbed her eyes before looking up at him with a grin. "It's snowing inside!" Before he could react, she picked up a handful of the "snow" and threw it into the air.

Zach sputtered as some of the flour puffed into his face. He looked down to survey the mess, but he couldn't scold Violet—

not when she was so excited. So, he knew there was only one reasonable thing to do. Following his daughter's example, Zach gathered a handful of flour from the counter and threw it into the air. "It's not just snowing. It's a blizzard!"

They both erupted into giggles and spun around in their floury wonderland.

Lia rang the doorbell for the second time, while balancing a cherry cheese pie in her free hand. Hearing rapid footsteps inside the house, she turned to smile at Nana. "I guess we shouldn't have come ten minutes early. Sounds like he's still busy."

"Maybe the doorbell is broken," Nana suggested. She knocked on the door.

"Be there in a second!" Zach's muffled voice called from inside. A few minutes later, the door opened, and an out of breath, disheveled version of Zach appeared. "Sorry for the wait. Violet and I had a little mishap in the kitchen. She just got out of the bath."

"That's all right. We're early." Lia grinned, noticing his hair had a white tinge to it, but she chose to keep the observation to herself.

Zach led the way into the kitchen. "The pizza has a few minutes left to cook. Please, feel free to sit at the breakfast bar while I finish the salad."

A few seconds after they sat down, Violet came dashing into the room in a yellow sundress, with her damp brown curls bouncing. "Luna, Lia...you're here!" The little girl dashed into Nana's arms first. "I missed you, Luna."

Nana grinned. "I missed you too, sweetheart. What have you been up to?"

Violet's eyes brightened. "We had a blizzard...in the house!" She spun around for emphasis.

Lia's eyebrow arched in amusement. "A blizzard?"

"A flour blizzard," the little girl said with a giggle before hugging Lia. "Daddy started it."

Lia peeked over at Zach, whose cheeks had taken on an adorable pink hue. "The flour tipped over and spilled all over Violet," he explained with a sheepish grin. "We made the best of the situation."

"After the blizzard we swept it all up and put the flour in a bag. Daddy said we're going to make homemade Play-Doh with it tomorrow."

"Yep, no point in wasting good flour right, pumpkin?"

Violet nodded as her grin grew even bigger.

"What a wonderful idea." Lia's heart warmed while continuing to watch Zach cut lettuce. She could tell he was an attentive dad by his sweet interactions with Violet, however, it was obvious the whole flour situation embarrassed him a bit. "Need help with the tomatoes?" Lia asked, changing the subject.

"Sure, that would be great. I need to check on the pizzas."

Lia came around the counter and started dicing the tomatoes. They were bright red on the inside, telling her they'd been ripened on the vine. "These look delicious. Did you buy them from a farmers' market? I didn't see one on the islands."

Zach shook his head and a hint of pride glimmered in his blue eyes. "Nope, those were homegrown out of our garden."

"Wow, so you're not only good with animals, but you have a green thumb, too."

"I don't know about that. We just grow a few things...tomatoes, cucumbers, peppers. Stuff like that. I tried spinach one time, and it was a catastrophe."

They shared a laugh before Lia turned her attention back to the tomatoes. "My dad enjoys gardening, too. I'm always amazed by what he grows. Unfortunately, I have trouble even keeping indoor potted plants alive."

Zach shrugged before opening the oven to inspect the pizzas. "It's been all about trial and error for us, but I was determined to grow natural and organic vegetables. It's good for Violet, and she enjoys tending the garden with me."

"That's wonderful. I bet she'll appreciate all you've taught her about growing things when she gets older. It's a good skill... one I wish I'd taken the time to learn."

"It's never too late to start. I'd be happy to give you a few pointers some time if you want. Even at Luna's apartment, you can grow a tomato plant in a bucket and set it on the front porch."

"I hadn't thought about that before. That's a good idea."

He grinned while tossing the different greens together in a large bowl. "You know, I have been thinking about starting a community garden here on the islands where folks can grow their own fruits and vegetables and maybe even selling the extra produce at a farmers' market type setting. I don't have enough space in my yard, but I'm in the process of scoping out a location."

"That sounds like a wonderful idea. I know I'd love not having to travel all the way to the mainland for my produce."

"That gives me hope some of the other residents would feel the same way."

"I'm sure they would." Lia watched Zach in amazement as he shared some ideas. A fire ignited in his eyes when he talked about it. She could sense he had a giving heart.

"You should contact Jace Young," Nana said from across the breakfast bar. "His property behind the Hopper Ear Apartments isn't being used for anything yet and I'm sure some of the older tenants would love to have a little garden plot to tend. It could also be a way for them to earn a little extra cash."

Zach's face lit up, and he rushed over to hug her. "Luna, you're so brilliant. I could kiss you!"

Nana chuckled as he released her. "I'm afraid I'm way too old for you, child. Even though it's hard to resist a silver fox." She winked.

He tilted his head to one side, blushing slightly again. "A silver fox? What are you talking about?"

She pointed toward his hair while stifling another laugh. "I wasn't going to say anything, but I couldn't help myself." She tilted her head toward the mirror on the opposite wall.

Zach crossed to his reflection and scoffed, seeing his hair powdered white. "Guess I was too busy getting everything ready to notice I'd aged twenty years!" He laughed and shook his head. "I'll be right back."

Lia scraped the chopped tomatoes into the salad bowl before watching Zach go out the glass sliding door and start fluffing the white powder from his hair. The chickens saw him come out and started running in from all corners of the yard. Apparently, they thought he had treats for them. They all tilted their heads as a cloud of white filtered from his brown hair. They eventually lost interest, except the black and white hen Lia remembered as Cookie. The bird tilted her head one way and then the other, observing Zach's odd behavior. A few moments later, when Zach came back in, Cookie strutted behind him like she belonged inside, too. When he swiftly closed the door behind him, the bird raised her head indignantly and pecked at the glass.

Zach with his hair going every which direction, ignored Cookie's antics and headed to wash his hands. At the same time the oven alarm went off for the pizza. "Well, the pizzas are done. I hope you're all hungry."

"I am!" Lia exclaimed with a wide grin, hoping it would help Zach feel less flustered. It was obvious he wasn't used to inviting people over for dinner, but he was a real trooper. There had been a few mishaps, but he managed it with grace and humor. If anything, the imperfections of the evening put her at ease. It showed Zach was genuine and real—a quality Lia had once thought illusive as sunshine on a stormy day. His girlfriend was a lucky woman.

What had changed? Zach watched Lia after dinner, noticing she was more relaxed and talkative than when they'd met a few days ago. Maybe Luna's presence made a difference. It was partly true he'd invited them to dinner so Violet could see Luna again. She was like a grandma to his little girl. However, now Zach realized he'd had other motivations, too.

Lia's brown eyes and long, dark lashes enchanted him as he listened to her talk. She told stories about when she visited her nana on Sparrow as a child. Violet drank it all in, still marveling at the fact Lia was Luna's granddaughter. All her curiosity about Lia's upbringing served as a stark reminder his daughter didn't have enough female role models in her life. Working from home had turned Zach a bit reclusive at times. He'd never given much thought to romantic relationships since becoming Violet's guardian. Had that been a mistake?

"Zach, have you shown Lia the garden path to your part of the beach yet?" Luna asked, drawing his attention back to the present.

"No, I guess I haven't." He turned to Lia. "Would you like to see it?"

Lia's eyes darted from her nana to Zach. "Oh, you don't have to go through all that trouble just for me."

He shook his head. "It's no trouble at all…that is, if you'd like to go."

"You really should, Lia," Luna encouraged. "It's one of the nicest views on the island."

She sighed and offered him a shy smile. "I guess a walk down to the beach would be nice."

Her hesitation made it painfully obvious she wasn't thrilled with Luna's idea, but Zach tiptoed around the fact. If playing dumb would earn him a walk to the beach with the lovely brown-eyed beauty across from him, he'd gladly accept the role.

9

*H*ow had she ended up in this awkward situation? Lia stared at her flip flops as she walked, concentrating on the way the sand crunched under her feet. Why would Nana betray her like this? She had to know Zach had a girlfriend—if not a fiancé—which was completely fine by Lia. It was Nana who'd made things awkward.

"Lia, is everything all right?"

She turned around and covered her mouth in embarrassment. She'd left poor Zach in the dust. "I'm sorry. You were nice enough to give me a tour, and I'm treating it like a quick window-shopping trip. Forgive me for being a little preoccupied."

He chuckled while catching up to her. "It's fine."

She continued on at a much slower pace and smiled at him. "This is really amazing. It makes me wonder if there's anything you're not good at. I mean...you're a gardener and animal rescuer by day and a hero who saves people stranded on the side of the road by night?"

He shrugged. "I don't know about all that. Actually, this garden was already here from the previous owner. It was quite the learning curve to learn how to care for all these plants, believe me. Also, there are plenty of things I'm not good at."

She lifted an amused eyebrow. "Like what?"

"Singing, for example. I start belting out a chorus and Colby howls up a storm."

She laughed. "Oh, I'm sure you're not that bad."

"Well, it's too much of a risk to those beautiful ears of yours to take the chance."

"Beautiful ears?" Lia shook her head with a giggle. "I've heard many smooth lines in my life, but that one's a first."

His cheeks reddened again, and Lia struggled to keep a straight face. "Sorry. I didn't mean it to sound that way."

"It's fine," she responded, deciding to let him off the hook. "I'm just giving you a hard time." She clasped her hands behind her back and moved closer to a group of white flowers with yellow centers, framed with mauve sepals. "Oh, I wish I had my camera. These are so pretty." She took out her phone and snapped a picture. "Do you know what they're called?"

"Purple Columbines. Violet loves them too because they're her favorite color. She calls them starlight flowers."

Lia put her phone away and reached out to touch one of the petals—taking care to not damage it. "Purple's my favorite, too."

"Violet will be excited to find out you have something in common. You know, she hasn't stopped talking about you since the other day."

Lia grinned. "She's such a sweetheart. Nana has been telling me so many stories about her. I'm so glad Violet likes to come over and keep her company."

"Well, I'm thankful for your nana. I don't have any family around here, but she kind of adopted Violet and I as her own."

"That sounds like something Nana would do," she agreed before they started walking again, this time side by side.

"You mentioned your camera. Are you a photographer?"

Lia shrugged. "It's a hobby mostly. I've taken portraits for my sister's family and my friends from time to time. I also like to take walks in nature and snap some shots of flowers and interesting trees...stuff like that."

His eyebrow arched. "I'd love to see your work."

She let out a nervous chuckle while waving away his suggestion. "It's not very good. Believe me, but I'd love to take some photography courses at some point. If I ever have enough money, that is."

"I'm sure you're better than you think."

She shrugged again. "Maybe." A few more flowers caught her attention as they walked, and Zach told her the names. It amazed her how much he knew. It was evident he'd spent countless hours on research to become an expert on the subject of gardening. Also, with the animals he rescued. She'd never met a man who paid so much attention to detail, and who used his intelligence to help creatures in need...and apparently people, too.

They walked until reaching the beach, where Zach motioned toward an area with some seating and a gazebo. "Here we are. I'd like to take credit for it all, but the previous homeowner built all this. I was just blessed enough to find this gem of a property. Violet really loves it here. It's challenging raising her on my own, but I couldn't ask for a better location to do it."

"It is lovely." Lia gazed out at the gentle waves with the afternoon sun glistening against them. She bit her lip to keep from asking him about Violet's mother. Had she passed away, or had they divorced? If it was the latter, was she still a part of their little girl's life?

The questions swirling in Lia's mind were none of her business, yet she couldn't stop from asking them in her mind. Lia was usually more direct, but something about Zach made her unusually shy. In truth, she admired him and it created inadequacy within her. He was about the same age as Lia, yet his life seemed so put together, even with the challenges that came with being a single dad. She didn't have nearly as many responsibilities, but lately her life felt like a speedboat captained by a crazy adrenaline junky, pulling her on water skis. No matter how hard she tried to motion for the boat to stop, it continued dragging her through choppy, turbulent waters.

"A pearl for your thoughts?"

Lia escaped the deep tidepool of thoughts invading her mind, noticing they'd made it to the gazebo. "What?"

"A pearl," Zach repeated, holding the glistening white ball with a violet tint. "Violet and I collect them, but I'm sure she wouldn't mind if you had one."

She smiled while taking it from him. "Thank you. It's beautiful."

Zach showed her a glass jar with a cork top filled with a variety of pearls. "Violet and I have a little collection going on here." He picked up the jar and tilted it from side to side, allowing the pearls to roll around inside it.

Lia marveled at the unique gems. "I had no idea they came in different colors."

Zach nodded with a grin. "Yep, I never thought of it either until we started our little collection." His eyes took on a thoughtful gleam. "And to think, they all started out when a tiny bit of sand wiggled its way into a clam shell."

"Amazing." Lia looked at the purple tinted pearl in her palm in wonder.

"Yeah," he agreed, moving a little closer. "I always tell Violet the pearls are like us. God makes every one of us unique. Even the difficult stuff we go through transforms us into the people we are meant to become."

"I never thought of it that way." Lia looked into Zach's sky-blue eyes, weakness pulling her like a rip current. How did he manage to reel her in so effortlessly? It was magical, yet infuriating. She didn't want to be reeled in. She wanted to resist him —avoid him at all costs. Falling for him was risky. It was reckless. It was…wrong. She'd been leaning into him without realizing, and now those amazing eyes were even closer. No. Lia backed up. "Um…I think we should go back now."

"Did I say something wrong?"

No, he'd said everything right. That was precisely the problem. "It's fine," she lied and turned to walk away.

"Lia," he called out and his hand grasped hers, bringing her to face him again. "Please, talk to me. I haven't known you for very long, but I can tell something's wrong."

Lia shook her head, eyes pricking with unwelcome tears. "You're a nice person, Zach, and I'm grateful for your help. I know you are used to rescuing lost sparrows, but you don't need to rescue me again. It's not fair. Not for either of us."

Zach's brow furrowed. "I don't understand. What's not fair?"

Lia sighed in exasperation. "I can't be the 'other woman.' That's not who I am. We can be friends, but that's as far as this thing's gonna go."

"Okay…friends is fine, but what *other woman*? It feels like we're on completely different pages."

"Obviously!" Lia closed her eyes, pinching the bridge of her nose while trying to organize her scrambled emotions. After a few moments, she looked back up at him, jaw set and ready to set the record straight. "I'm happy for you and I won't be that person that splits up a couple. I just won't do it. I hope you understand."

"A couple?"

"Yeah, you and that redhead. Your girlfriend. I saw you with her in front of your house yesterday."

Zach's deer in the headlights look faded and then he chuckled, infuriating Lia even further. "Kendall? Now I see what's going on."

She braced her hands on her hips. "And what's that?"

Zach's face sobered as he met her gaze again. "Kendall is the local veterinarian and a good friend. I helped her debug her website yesterday."

Lia's cheeks flooded with warmth as she snuck a peek in his direction. "So, she's not your girlfriend?"

A sheepish grin lit up his face, and he scratched his head. "Nope, haven't had one of those in ages."

Stifling a gasp with her hand, she stepped a little closer, mortified at her mistake. "Zach, I'm so sorry. I don't know how I got so mixed up."

He waved away her apology. "Anyone could have made the same mistake."

"You mean, anyone as nosey as I am?"

He chuckled with a playful wink. "Yeah, guess you could say that."

Feeling her shoulders relax, Lia laughed with him, all the while amazed by the change in mood. How did Zach manage to do it? He'd taken a tense situation where she could have died of embarrassment and flipped it into something lighthearted and humorous. It was as incredible as one of those house flipper shows she enjoyed watching.

After a few moments, Zach stopped laughing and gazed down at her, sweeping away a few strands of hair from her forehead. Her heart pounded as their eyes met. "You know, when the sun hits your eyes at just the right angle, they have a little green in them."

Lia continued gazing at him, her previous embarrassment sifting away like sand through her fingers. What was her excuse to stay away from Zach now? He was too nice? Too much of a gentleman? That would be something, wouldn't it? In all honesty, Lia had tended to go for the bad boys in the past. It was like a magnetic pull or something, although she didn't notice they were bad until it was too late. Zach was different. Maybe, just maybe, could she fall for a good guy for a change?

10

*H*opper Ear Cove. Such an interesting name. Zach studied the map on his GPS while the ferry transported Lia's car to Hooper Island. He chuckled to himself, realizing the location of the apartment complex was located on part of the island shaped like two rabbit ears. His destination was on the left ear in a small cove.

"Why are we in Lia's car, Daddy?"

Zach grinned into the rear-view mirror, realizing Violet had woken up from her nap. "Because I fixed it, and Lia needs it back now."

Violet scrunched her nose. "But how will we get home? Will we have to walk?"

"No, I talked to Jace, and he's going to give us a ride home from Hopper."

"Does the Easter Bunny live on Hopper?"

Zach chuckled. "I don't think so, pumpkin. He probably has a secret island somewhere so no one can find him."

"Are you sure?" she asked, her eyes suspicious. "I bet Alicia would know better since she lives there."

Zach scoffed playfully. "So, you'd believe her more than me? Am I chopped liver now?"

Violet giggled. "Daddy, you're not liver. That's gross."

He laughed at her expression, laced with half amusement and half disgust. "I'm not talking about actual liver, sweetie. It's just an expression."

"What's an expression?"

He let out a sigh as the ferry neared the slip at Hopper. "Just silly phrases adults say that mean something else."

"I don't get it."

Zach grinned again. "You will when you're bigger."

"When I'm old like you?"

He struggled to hold back a laugh at her brutal honesty. Kids were good at that. "Yep, when you're old like me," he answered, changing the subject before he dug himself any deeper into a hole. "So, when we get there, you can play with Alicia while I talk to her husband, Jace, okay?"

Violet nodded in the rear-view mirror, her eyes glowing with excitement. "Okay Daddy! Will Lia be there too? I'd like to play with her again."

"I'm not sure, pumpkin." Zach paused before driving onto the road toward Hopper Ear Cove, remembering his encounter with Lia a few days ago. After their misunderstanding about him having a girlfriend, she'd really calmed down and even opened up to him a little. Somehow it reminded him of a butterfly beginning to emerge from a chrysalis. She'd gone from guarded, to revealing some of her passions, like photography. Seeing her snap dozens of flower pictures along the garden path was a memory he enjoyed recalling. Her curiosity about the flower names was intriguing, and the fact she appreciated his knowledge of the subject. Her brown eyes lit up with wonder, causing her inner beauty to shine through as well.

After the time they spent together, he was left with curiosity about her. Why didn't she pursue photography professionally? Why was she so critical of her abilities? They were puzzling questions—ones he hoped would be answered soon.

When they arrived at the apartment complex, Jace and Alicia came out to greet them, along with Jace's retired service dog, Cooper. Alicia took Violet on a walk around the complex. Jace shook Zach's hand as they left. "So glad you came up with this idea of having a community garden. I don't know why my dad and I didn't think about having one before. It's a great idea, and I think the residents will love it."

"Yeah, I hope they do."

They walked down the path toward a hill, in search of a good location for the gardens with Jace's golden retriever trailing close behind. All the while, Zach kept glancing off to the left where the apartments were located. Which number did Luna live in? He couldn't recall. Still, he kept hoping to see Lia appear. If she wasn't home, he'd just leave the car in one of the parking spaces behind Luna's apartment and let her know it was there.

Lia hadn't called since their dinner on Sunday, but he'd thought of her often. Did the job at Kendall's mobile clinic work out? He was halfway tempted to call her and ask but decided against the idea. He'd provided the connection to inquire about the job, but it was none of his business whether Lia decided to take it or not.

As they climbed the hill and approached a flat plateau, Zach steered his preoccupied thoughts back to the subject at hand. He looked around the area, imagining the possibilities. "This has potential. Plenty of space and sunshine." He pointed a little to the left. "There's also an area with half shade over there to plant the peas and stuff like that so they don't get scorched on the vine."

Jace smiled while surveying the area. "Yeah, my thought

exactly." He leaned down to pat Cooper on the head. "Now the next step is collecting enough money to make it all happen. I've got some to contribute, but it's going to take more for lumber, dirt, tools, and a watering system. I think the older people would appreciate raised beds to plant in as well."

Zach nodded. "I agree. And not just them. My back would appreciate it, too." They shared a laugh before he continued. "I have some money to contribute to the project, and I think my church would contribute. For the rest, maybe we could talk to the island council and see about a grant, or we could do fundraisers...or a combination of both."

"Sounds like a plan. When were you wanting to start on this?"

A grin tugged on his lips. "As soon as possible. I'm a proactive kind of guy, you might say."

"Nothing wrong with that." Jace chuckled, straightening to his full height. "Well, let's go back to the office and start drawing up some plans."

Lia returned to the apartment complex with a grin a mile wide. Her interview with Kendall Mulligan had gone perfectly, ending in a job offer. It was part time only, but she was thrilled to have the position. While she stayed with Nana, she could contribute with the rent and food. Hopefully she'd also have enough to save each month. She'd also have time to think about what kind of permanent job she wanted someday.

That Sunday she'd gone to church with Nana. It had been the first time she'd been in a long time. Lia thought she'd be bored out of her mind or feel judged, but she'd been wrong on both accounts. The people were very kind and understanding toward her. Plus, the preacher's sermon on Mathew 6:34 had clicked with her. The pastor said worrying about tomorrow only steals your joy for today. It made her realize she'd been spending far too much time worrying and stressing over her future. While sitting in the pew, she recommitted her life to God and decided to let Him handle her current circumstances. Now, it was obvious to her that He'd been working behind the scenes on her behalf. He had provided her a job. Also, after Nana bragged about her photography while there, she had several members of the congregation interested in family photo shoots. If that was a sign of the direction things were going, Lia had more confidence other aspects of her life would change for the better too.

When she arrived at Nana's apartment, the older woman was resting in the recliner with her feet up. She lifted her head when Lia entered and offered a bright smile. "Oh, there you are. How did it go?"

Lia almost burst with the news she'd been holding in since the interview. "I got the job!"

"That's wonderful! When do you start?"

Lia hugged Nana and pulled over an ottoman to sit across from her. "Kendall says she needs me right away. They are swamped with extra vet calls and the paperwork that comes with it, so I'm starting tomorrow."

"I'm so happy for you, Lia...and even if it's a little selfish on my part, I'm glad you're staying longer."

Happy tears filled Lia's eyes as she squeezed her nana's hand. "I'm glad, too. I didn't realize how much I've missed you until I came for this visit. I love it here on the islands."

Nana wiped tears of her own. "You can stay as long as you like, dear. Your company does my heart good."

A knock on the door interrupted the moment and Lia went to answer it. Her mouth hinged open when Zach appeared on the porch. "Um...hi," she managed as his blue eyes gazed into hers.

"Sorry for showing up unannounced," he said while fidgeting with a business card in his hand. "I came to drop off your car and talk with Jace."

Lia's brain unscrambled enough for her to produce a lucid sentence. "It's okay. You just caught me by surprise." She peeked around the door in curiosity. "Where's Violet?"

He motioned toward the office. "Alicia is watching her for a few minutes."

"Oh, ok." Lia stood in the doorway, fidgeting with the handle. What was wrong with her? She'd never been so tongue-tied in her life. In the absence of Violet saying adorable things to break the tension, she didn't know what to say next.

"Anyway," Zach finally said. "I don't mean to pry, but how did the interview go?"

Her shoulders relaxed, resuming her happy frame of mind from earlier. "It went great, thanks to you...and God. I start tomorrow."

"That's wonderful news." His eyes twinkled. "I'm praying the job is a blessing for you, Lia." He reached in his pocket and handed her car keys. "Here you go. Your car should work good as new now."

"Thank you again. How much do I owe you?"

He put his hand out to stop her. "You don't owe me a thing. The part didn't cost much."

"Are you sure?"

"Yep, I won't take no for an answer." He stepped back, looking toward the office. "Well, Jace offered to drive Violet and I back home. I don't want to keep him waiting. See you later."

"Yeah, see ya. And thanks again." Lia watched him walk away before shutting the door and leaning her back against it with a sigh.

"Who was that, Lia?" Nana called from the living room.

She bit her lip to ward off a silly grin. "It was Zach. He

dropped off the car and stopped by to see how the interview went."

"That was nice of him. You should have invited him in."

"He couldn't stay. Seemed like he was in a hurry."

"I see. Well, maybe next time."

Nana sounded satisfied, so Lia crossed the kitchen and filled the sink with soapy water to wash a few dishes. Picking up the first cup, she scoffed in exasperation. The glass was tinted almost the shade of Zach's eyes. Why could she not get this guy out of her head? Lia picked up the glass again when there was another knock on the door. She dried off her hands and went to the door again with a furrowed brow.

"Hi again," Zach said when Lia opened it. "Sorry, you probably think I'm a weirdo now."

No actually, she thought his awkwardness was kind of adorable. "You're not weird," she said instead, unable to keep from smiling. "Forget something?"

"Yeah." He let out an anxious chuckle and raked his fingers through his hair. "I forgot to ask you something."

"Sure, what's that?"

"Would you like to go out to dinner this Saturday?"

Lia stared at him with wide eyes. Had he really just asked her out?

"Yes!" Nana's voice called from the living room. "Of course she'll go!"

Lia rolled her eyes playfully and nodded. "What time?"

Zach sighed, and a radiant smile bloomed on his lips. "How about I'll pick you up around five? That way we'll have time for ferry travel and be eating around six."

"Sounds perfect."

After Zach left, Lia came back in, met with Nana's probing eyes. "Sooo, what did you say?"

"Well, after we were so rudely interrupted..." she teased with an amused raise of one eyebrow. She attempted to keep from smiling but failed miserably. "I said yes."

Nana grinned from ear to ear. "Good. Have I said before just how much I like that young man?"

Lia nodded. "Yes, several times, but that's all right. I like him, too."

11

*K*endall watched the ice in her glass of iced tea slowly dissolve, like her hopes of hearing from Tyler that week. Lunch at Tiff's house was supposed to be a relaxing time for some girl talk, but she couldn't manage to concentrate. Every morning that week she started the day with hope she'd hear from him, but when the night fell, she went to bed restless. By the time Friday afternoon rolled around, marking two weeks since they'd talked, she was entertaining her worst fears of what may have happened to him.

"I'm sure it's probably nothing," Tiff commented from across the table. "The last time he was on tour there were times when I didn't hear from him for several weeks at a time. It usually just meant his squadron was on the move or ended up somewhere remote without access to phone or internet. Right before that would happen, he'd say something silly in code at the end of the email or letter like 'Saw a flying squirrel today' or 'Gotta pack my superman cape.' Some sort of hint to give me a heads up without saying it directly. I don't remember him saying anything this time, but I could have missed it."

"I never realized he did that." Kendall tried to be positive but she couldn't manage to smile at Tyler's sister. A pang of jealousy rose within her like a rogue wave. He had a secret code with Tiff. Why not her? Didn't he realize how much she'd worry?

Tiff placed her hand over Kendall's and the knowing look in her friend's eyes suddenly made her want to cry. "I know how stressful it is not knowing, but we have to put the safety of our loved ones in God's hands. Will and I had this discussion before he left to go on tour. He knew the risks and didn't want to leave me and the kids, but felt called into the service...like God had a higher purpose for him out there. When he didn't come home..." Tiff paused for a moment to wipe her moist cheeks. "When he didn't come home, I doubted. I was so angry at God."

Unrelenting guilt broke through Kendall's jealousy. "I'm sorry, Tiff. I'm such a nervous wreck. Here I am whining about Tyler not contacting me for a few weeks, and you must be thinking about when you lost Will. Please forgive me for being insensitive."

Tiff shook her head and managed a smile through her tears. "There's nothing to forgive. You're a nervous wreck because you care about my brother. Honestly, I think you love him as much as I loved Will. It blesses my heart to know Tyler found someone wonderful like you."

"Thank you for saying that. I do love him. More than I ever dreamed I could love someone." Kendall wiped away tears of her own. "How do you stay so strong, Tiff?"

Tiff shrugged. "I don't feel very strong, but God helps me get out of bed every day when sometimes I just want to lie there and be swallowed by grief. Things were worse before Tyler came home. He told me how Will went above and beyond to make a difference over there..." Her lips trembled as she continued speaking. "His last act on earth was to shield children who would have died in that horrible explosion. It made me realize his death wasn't in vain. There was a purpose for it. I may never understand completely, but one day in heaven I will.

Most of all, I'm comforted by something my mom used to say. Death isn't really 'goodbye' for those who know Christ. It's just 'see you later.'"

"That's beautiful." Kendall sniffled and moved to hug Tiff. They cried until their torrent of emotions were spent. Afterward, she sat back in her chair with a sigh. "It's good to cry sometimes."

Tiff nodded. "Especially with a good friend." She raised an eyebrow. "And…one day a sister-in-law, right?"

"If he gets around to asking me."

Her friend's smile widened, as if picturing the future. "He will, believe me. I know my brother, and it won't take him long after he comes back."

"More than anything, I just want him to come home safely." Kendall fidgeted with the opal promise ring on her right hand, imagining what it would be like seeing Tyler drop to one knee and pop the question. Was she ready for that? A wave of realization washed over her. If Tyler's absence from the past months taught her anything, it was that she never wanted to be separated from him again. Yes, she was ready to make that commitment whenever and wherever he asked her.

After her lunch with Tiff, Kendall went back to the mobile clinic parked on Merriweather a few miles away. She felt more peace about the situation with Tyler. His safety was in God's hands, and she knew worrying wouldn't help.

When she entered the RV, Alicia was at the front desk, helping train their new secretary on some of their new computer software. Both women looked up from their task to smile when Kendall approached. "How was your lunch?" Alicia asked.

"Good. How's the training going?"

"Excellent! Lia is the perfect student."

Lia scoffed playfully. "I don't know about perfect, but I think

I'm getting the hang of it. I used to use similar software at my previous job."

"Well, I'm glad. I knew you'd be a good fit for this job."

A few clients filtered in with their pets during the rest of the afternoon, and Kendall entrusted Alicia with helping Lia learn the ropes. In between patients, she was pleased to see Lia doing most of the computer work on her own and only having to stop occasionally to ask Alicia a question. A weight lifted off her shoulders. Since expanding vet services to all the islands, Kendall went home in the evenings buried in paperwork to go through after dinner. Her sister, Carly, used to help, but was too busy traveling the globe with her billionaire husband. Now with Lia taking care of it, Kendall would have less stress. Maybe she'd even put her feet up and enjoy a bowl of chocolate chip cookie dough ice cream in the evenings occasionally. It was a comforting thought.

Prompted by Tatertot's cascade of excited meowing, Lia leaned down and scooped the tabby cat into her arms. "Miss me? I love you, too, handsome boy," she cooed while cuddling him close to her. After a few moments, Lia sat Tatertot on the floor and poured food into his bowl.

After he started eating while emitting contented purrs, Lia came back into the living room and stretched out on the sofa. She managed a drowsy smile in Nana's direction. "So, what would you think of going out for dinner tonight? Granny's has some really good fried chicken and mashed potatoes. It tasted just like a home-cooked meal."

"Sure. That sounds good." Nana relaxed her head against the recliner with a sigh.

Lia studied her with a furrowed brow. "Are you feeling all right, Nana? You look worn out."

Nana waved away her concern. "I'm fine. I think I just overdid things while quilting today. I'll perk up before dinner. Think I'll just take a little cat nap here before we go."

"Why don't you take a nap in the bedroom instead? I'll call for a takeout order and bring it home."

Nana fought a yawn as she started to get up. "All right. That sounds like a good idea."

After she left the room, Lia made the call to Granny's and then relaxed back on the couch. She kept her phone in her hand and started checking her emails. Tatertot jumped onto her stomach and started kneading. Lia groaned and petted the cat. "Okay, that's enough, boy. My muscles will turn into dough if you knead them anymore. Tatertot continued despite her protests. Lia finally had to intervene and moved the cat to a spot beside her instead. She stroked his fluffy orange ears to keep him happy as her phone buzzed. Seeing Zach's message, heat tingled in her cheeks.

DATE STILL ON?

Lia Grinned before texting back. YEP, I'LL BE READY AT 5 SHARP.

LOOKING FORWARD TO IT. MAKE SURE TO WEAR OLDER CLOTHES YOU DON'T MIND GETTING DIRTY.

Lia paused at the odd request. She'd already had a cute little purple dress picked out, but she'd have to scratch that idea. K... WHERE ARE WE GOING?

SORRY, THAT INFORMATION IS CLASSIFIED.

OH, I SEE HOW IT IS. Lia rolled her eyes but couldn't rein in the goofy grin ransoming her face. What kind of crazy date did Zach have planned?

LOL..SEE YOU TOMORROW.

K. SEE YA.

Lia put the phone down with a silent giggle as Tatertot climbed onto her stomach, proceeding to knead her ab muscles into mush again. This time, she was too distracted to care. She hated surprises, but with Zach, it was different. Although she'd only known Zach for a couple of weeks, she trusted him more than other guys she'd dated. The thought of the mysterious date where she had to wear older clothes she didn't mind ruining, both drove her crazy and filled her heart with joyous anticipation. What on earth was he planning? Thoughts about sports involving mud swirled through her mind. Four wheeling or dirt bike riding maybe? Whatever it was, she couldn't wait.

Kendall arrived on her street, mouth already watering in anticipation of her ice cream dessert. Maybe just this once she'd eat her ice cream first and then have dinner. That was a brilliant idea if she'd ever heard one. After all, she had to celebrate that the new secretary was doing such a wonderful job.

Smiling, she stopped at the mailbox at the end of her driveway. Before pulling in, she filtered through the bills and junk mail. At the very bottom was a letter with familiar handwriting on it. It was sent several weeks before, but it still provided hope.

"Tyler," she whispered and hugged the letter close, imagining their love could span the ocean of distance between them. "I hope wherever you are, you can feel my love. Stay safe and come home to me." Her tear-filled eyes shifted to the sky. "God, please protect my brave Marine."

*a*licia rushed around the apartment, getting a few last things organized before their guests arrived. As she reached for the cleaner spray to wash a window she'd missed, Jace came from behind and wrapped his arm around her.

"Try to relax. The apartment doesn't have to be spotless," he encouraged. "Remember, we're entertaining a four-year-old for a few hours. Not the Queen of England."

Alicia melted into her husband's embrace with a giggle. "You have a good point. Sorry for going overboard. Maybe I'm just a little nervous. When Zach asked us, I couldn't say no. I mean, Violet is so adorable, but now I'm wondering what I've gotten myself into."

"Things seemed to go well the other day when you took her for a walk around the grounds."

Alicia nodded against him. "Yeah, it did, but that was only for about thirty minutes. What happens when she gets bored or starts crying because she misses her dad?" She released a deep sigh. "I wish I knew more about kids. I didn't have any younger siblings, and my niece is only a few months old. That's a big disadvantage, you know?"

"Alicia, look at me."

She did as he asked and turned to face him. There were so many things she loved about Jace, but his calming hazel eyes were her favorite. They peeled back the layers of anxiety, revealing her soul underneath. His gaze was never judgmental or condescending—only full of love and understanding. Looking into his eyes now, she felt safe and understood.

"We're a team, remember?" After she nodded, he went on. "I'm not saying there won't be a few bumps along the way, but we'll figure this out together. After all, we're kind of in the same boat since I was an only child. Kids are a bit of a mystery to me too, but I'm up for the challenge if you are."

Alicia grinned up at him as her apprehension began to melt away. "I am."

He pulled her close again, allowing Alicia to hear his steady heartbeat. "This will be a good experience for one day when we have kids of our own."

Her heartbeat quickened as she leaned back to look at him. "Have you thought a lot about starting a family?"

Jace shrugged and smoothed back her long hair. "From time to time I think about a little girl toddling around our place who looks just like you."

"Or maybe a little future baseball player who looks like you?"

His arms wrapped around her waist again. "Who says we can't have one of each? After we finish the house, we'll have plenty of room."

"I wouldn't object." She kissed him and chuckled softly as possibilities grew in her mind. Before meeting Jace, she imagined a conversation like this would be terrifying. Now, married and making plans to restore and move into Jace's grandparents' house on the lookout, talking about future children felt like the next step. Most people wanted to wait a few years after marriage, but Alicia thought of it as an adventure. Especially after Jace's brain surgery to treat his seizures last year. It reminded both of them that life was a precious and sometimes fragile blessing. No one knew how long it would last, so it was best to live each moment to the fullest.

Jace released her to check his watch. "Well, they should be here any minute. I better start on some mac and cheese. Zach said it was Violet's favorite meal."

Alicia planted her hands on her hips. "Oh, so you got some insider tips, huh?"

"Yeah." He grinned at her again. "Try not to stress. If we have questions tonight, Mrs. Diaz is right up the path. She knows Violet pretty well, doesn't she?"

She nodded. "Yeah, they were neighbors before Luna moved here."

"See? Everything's gonna be fine."

The doorbell rang, and Alicia playfully arched her eyebrow at Jace. "Ready or not, here she comes!"

If Zach thought Violet wouldn't want to part with him for the night, he would have been wrong. She ran inside the Young's apartment and practically squealed Alicia's name as she leapt into her arms. The next thing she noticed was the mac and cheese. Zach chuckled while saying bye and kissing the top of his daughter's head. "I'll be back around nine."

"All right. Have a good evening," Jace said before Zach walked out the door and closed it behind him.

The short walk to Luna's apartment didn't provide enough time for him to gather his thoughts, so he stood by the door for a minute to catch his breath. He hadn't played the dating game since Violet toddled into his life and was severely out of practice. What could he say to break the ice? Maybe something funny?

While still formulating a plan, the door swung open, and he

stood face to face with Lia. Her eyes widened as she stepped back. "Zach! Sorry, did you ring the bell? I didn't hear it. I was just coming out to wait for you."

A nervous chuckle escaped his lips. "I hadn't rung it yet," he admitted, not sure what else to say. Lia wore an oversized purple t-shirt, dipping off one shoulder and the bottom tied to one side with a black tank top underneath. Her jeans had tears at the knees and were stained with splatters of multi-colored paint.

"These are my paint clothes from when I gave my apartment a makeover," she told him, noticing him scanning her outfit. She bit her lip when he didn't say anything back. "You said to wear something old, right?"

"Yeah, that'll work fine." Zach snapped out of his awkward stupor. To be honest, Lia looked drop dead gorgeous in whatever she wore, but tonight, she rocked an eighties style look with class. "Are you ready to go?"

"Yeah, just let me say a quick bye to Nana and grab my purse." Within a few minutes, they were heading to the parking lot. Lia stopped to stare at his white Camaro. "I thought you had an SUV?"

He grinned while opening the passenger-side door for her. "I do, but this is my other car. One of the only possessions from my bachelor lifestyle in the city. It sounds silly, but I haven't had the heart to sell it yet. I mostly just take it out for Sunday drives if it's nice out. Violet likes it with the convertible top down so she can feel the wind in her hair. She says it's like flying in an airplane."

She chuckled with a nod. "Oh, I see. Well, I'm not complaining. It's a nice car."

"Thanks." After closing her door and climbing into the driver's side, Zach noticed Lia still attempting to hide a goofy grin as he put on his seat belt. "What is it? Did I do something wrong?"

"It's nothing really...I guess it's been a long time since a guy opened a door for me."

He frowned. "I'm sorry. My uncle raised me the old-fashioned way. I realize some women may find the custom offensive."

Her hand touched his, and she shook her head, grinning even bigger. "Well, I don't. I find it endearing, really. Who says a woman can't be strong, independent, *and* treated like a princess at the same time?"

"Well said." Zach's shoulders relaxed as he drove out of the parking lot. Maybe dating hadn't changed as much as he feared...at least when he dated someone like Lia. The more he got to know her, the more he realized she was one of a kind.

By the time they arrived at their destination, the sun had begun setting. Zach parked at a little waterfront seafood grill with outdoor seating. Lia couldn't keep herself from staring at the gorgeous views as the hostess led them to their seats. Soft calypso music played in the background, adding to the lighthearted, carefree ambiance of seaside life.

"I know this place doesn't look like much," Zach said. "But it has the best appetizers I've ever tasted. The fried clams are my favorite."

"I've never tried those before, but I've always wanted to, and this restaurant is charming. I love supporting small local businesses. Most of the time, they have better service and more authentic food than the big franchises can offer."

Zach nodded with a grin. "I agree. When Violet and I first moved to the area, a friend from church suggested this place. It's not fancy by any means, but you can tell it's fresh. That makes all the difference."

After placing their orders, they continued making small talk while enjoying all the sounds and sights the evening had to offer with the sound of waves crashing on the shore and crickets chirping in the background. Lia discovered she enjoyed being with Zach as much as when Violet was around. He had a pleasant manner about him that put her at ease. She'd thought the secretive location of their date would drive her crazy, but now, she hardly thought of it. Instead, Lia savored every moment, drinking in each word Zach spoke.

When the delicious appetizer of fried clams arrived, Lia snagged the opportunity to cast the conversation into a more personal direction. "So, earlier you mentioned your uncle raised you the old-fashioned way? Would you like to tell me more about him?"

"Sure." Zach took a drink of sweet tea before going on. "I went to live on his farm after my mother passed away. I was about sixteen at the time and didn't have anywhere else to go. He became a father figure to me." His gaze dropped to the table. "Unfortunately, my real dad was never around."

"I'm sorry to hear that."

Zach shrugged and met her eyes again. "It was a difficult season of my life, but I'm thankful my uncle was there when I needed him. He grew sweet potatoes and taught me everything he knew about farming. It was hard work, but it was good for me, and I learned a lot of good values from him."

"Sounds like you had an interesting upbringing."

"Yeah, I did. I think my uncle hoped I'd take over the family business, but I had other dreams for my future. He understood and gave me his blessing when it was time for me to leave for college."

"So, what made you choose web design?"

Zach rubbed his chin thoughtfully. "I guess learning about technology and computers has been something I've been interested in since childhood. My mom always encouraged my sister and I to go for our dreams, so I was determined to do just that."

"That's a wonderful way to keep her memory alive. So, did your sister take to farm life also?"

Zach's smile faded as he fiddled with the tablecloth. "At first, but my sister has always been wild at heart. My uncle wasn't sure how to handle a rebellious teenager. He'd never had any kids of his own. I tried my best to help keep her out of trouble, but she ran away from my uncle's and ended up living with some friends who were a bad influence." Zach looked up at her with sadness and regret radiating through his eyes. "She's been in and out of drug rehab a few times. I try to keep in contact as much as I can, but she moves around a lot."

"I'm sorry to hear that."

Zach nodded and managed a smile. "I keep praying God will turn her heart around. I'll never give up hope."

"That's the best thing any of us can do. I know Nana always prays for me and I can't tell you how many times I've needed the extra prayers in the situations I get myself into. My antics drive Mia crazy." She chuckled softly.

Soon the waiter came with their main dish, providing the perfect opportunity for a change of subject after Zach prayed over the meal. "I know from my conversations with Luna you have a big family," Zach said. "Do you keep in contact with them?"

Lia nodded with a grin. "Yeah, I try to, but it became more difficult after getting my job at the magazine. I have two sisters and an older brother. Then there's all our extended family. My father side is Puerto Rican and my mother's side is from the States. It made for some pretty interesting family get-togethers growing up."

Zach smiled. "I can imagine. Do you still have them often?"

Lia shook her head. "Not so much anymore. My parents divorced when I was seventeen. After that, the family kind of split apart."

"Sorry to hear that."

She shrugged, painting on a fake smile. "I'm sure some people have had it worse off than I have. We have our feuds, but at least I have my sisters, brother, and father. My mother and I rarely speak, but maybe with time that'll change."

Zach nodded, and they continued eating their meal, mostly in silence, with Lia lost in her own thoughts. It had been a long time since she'd talked about her family, but somehow Zach had drawn it out of her. He wasn't pushy like some guys she'd dated, but when she spoke, he really listened, which was a rare quality. He also made himself vulnerable by sharing some difficult things from his own past. Lia fought the urge to ask him more—like the subject of Violet's mom. However, she decided to wait. Their conversation had been pretty deep for a first date so far. Lia wanted to switch gears and lighten things up a bit.

After ordering some fried cheesecake bite for dessert, Lia felt like the old grandfather clock in her Nana's dining room. If she was wound up any tighter, her spring would break loose. She leaned toward Zach with an arched eyebrow. "So, are you going to tell me where we're going for the second part of our date or not?"

"I'll give you a clue." His boyish grin reminded her of the time her three-year-old nephew drew all over the living room wall when she came over for Thanksgiving. Lia had struggled not to laugh at the time, but her older sister was furious.

"And what's that?" she prompted.

"It's only a short walk from here."

Lia turned to the right, noticing a little Italian restaurant. That couldn't be it. However, to the left she read a sign. A grin spread across her face. "Paintball? Is that the secret?"

A boyish smile graced his face again. "How do you know it's not laser tag? That's on the sign, too, you know."

Lia chuckled and tugged at one sleeve of her shirt. "Judging from the wardrobe you suggested, my best guess is paintball."

"Have you ever played before?"

Lia nodded and then shook her head before covering her mouth to suppress some giggles. "Yes and no. Ask Nana and she'll say I shot blueberry paintballs all over her living room floor. That's about all the experience I have."

"I'd love to hear the story behind that."

"Maybe sometime."

He arched one brow. "So, are you up for some paintball?"

She stared at him for a few moments in astonished silence. Few guys surprised her, but Zach had done it several times since they met. Why was she surprised their first date would be just as unorthodox as everything else in their relationship? Wasn't that what impressed her so much about Zach in the first place? Lia gathered her thoughts and nodded as her heart pumped with adrenaline. "Yeah, of course I am."

13

*T*wo hours later, Zach stood beside Lia on the ferry, under an ocean of stars. Some people gawked at their paint splattered appearance, but he didn't care. It had been a fun date, and Lia impressed him by being an excellent shot during their paintball war.

"Sorry I got you in the ear," she said with a giggle.

Zach rubbed his sore ear. "It's all right. No harm done." He refrained from telling her his hearing in that ear was still muffled. There was no need to make her feel guilty over something that would go away in a few hours…hopefully anyway.

"You've still got some blue paint splattered on your earlobe."

He tried to rub it away with his fingers. "There, is it gone now?"

Lia giggled again. "No. Here, let me help." She took out a wet wipe she'd saved from the restaurant and gently rubbed the paint off. "There, that's better."

With Lia so close, Zach noticed her lavender perfume, drawing him in. When her brown eyes met his, he reached to touch a green splotch on her cheek. "You still have some paint on you too."

She grinned. "I don't have any wipes left. Guess I'll have to wash it off at home."

"It looks good on you anyway." They shared a laugh before both turning serious. Zach's hand remained on Lia's cheek and he didn't move it. The way her brown eyes twinkled in the moonlight made his heart thunder like a summer storm, but he held back. The spark between them had ignited quickly, but he wasn't looking for a fling. With Violet in his life, he needed someone who'd be willing to make a long-term commitment someday. Time and patience would show him if Lia was that woman. It was best to take their relationship slow. Zach dropped his hand from her cheek and took a step back, smiling. "Sorry, this date was so...unconventional."

She arched an amused eyebrow. "It was fun. Besides, conventional dates are overrated."

He chuckled. "So, for our second date..."

"You're already thinking of a second date?" she interrupted. "What did you have in mind?"

"Skydiving?"

Lia's eyes widened in mock horror. "I think I'd prefer to keep my feet on solid ground."

"Okay, so no extreme dating. I hear ya. I'm not a big fan of heights, either." He tapped his bearded chin, enjoying teasing her a little. "Would kayaking off of Mimosa be a possibility? Or does that go against your feet on solid ground rule?"

She grinned up at him. "I wasn't thinking about water when I said that. Actually, kayaking sounds like a good compromise to me, but won't it be a little cold for a spring date?"

"There are wetsuits for rent there. Trust me, it's fun."

"Okay, sounds like a plan."

Lia's eyes shot open for the third time while waiting for the church service to start, and she casually glanced around her to see if anyone had taken notice of her snoozing. Seeing other congregants still fellowshipping with others in the pews around them, she let out a relieved sigh. Lia took a large gulp of coffee from her insulated mug, hoping the caffeine would help her stay awake during the service.

"Are you all right, dear?" Nana asked from beside her.

Lia nodded. "Yeah, I just didn't get much sleep last night."

Nana frowned in concern. "I'm sorry to hear that. Maybe an air mattress would be better than that sofa bed. We should look into buying one."

"No, the sofa bed is just fine, really. I just had a lot on my mind. I'll take a nap when we get home."

Her words calmed Nana's concern, giving Lia an excuse to dissolve into her own thoughts again. Really, she should have had plenty of time to sleep if her mind would have allowed her to do so. Zach had taken her back to Hopper Ear Cove around ten. She'd wanted to fold out the sofa bed and go right to sleep, but she had to wash off the paint. Lia had been so exhausted—it was all she could manage not to fall asleep in the shower. However, the moment her head hit the pillow, her mind had taken off like a race car with the gas pedal stuck to the floorboard. The date had been amazing. She'd been out on several "traditional" dinner and movie dates with guys where she'd been bored out of her mind, ended up having to pay because the guy "forgot his wallet," or any number of mishaps. Zach's unconventional date had pleasantly surprised her. He'd kept her attention the entire time with humor and meaningful conversation. She found herself wishing the nearly perfect night could have lasted longer.

Only one moment kept replaying in her mind and keeping her awake. For one moment on the ferry ride back to Hooper, Lia thought Zach was about to kiss her, but he hesitated. She kept telling herself it was only their first date, and she should be grateful he was acting like a gentleman. However, she couldn't stop imagining how a kiss would have been the perfect ending to the date. Oh, how she'd longed for him to kiss her!

Lia came out of her brain fog as Kendall and a couple she didn't know sat in the pew ahead of her. They turned around and greeted her. "Lia, I'd like you to meet my sister, Carly, and this is her husband, Jean-Luc. They just returned from Paris."

"It's nice to meet you both." She gulped down her nerves, remembering Kendall talking about Carly and her French husband. With pictures of the billionaire couple's extravagant wedding plastered all over news, Lia was surprised she'd never put two and two together. Was she really sitting behind the famous Jean Luc Belshaw and his wife? They gave her warm greetings and didn't seem to pick up on her anxiety. The couple were both down to earth which was a pleasant surprise.

After they turned back around in their seats, Alicia and Jace scooted in next to her. Alicia gave Lia a hug. "Welcome back! I'm so glad you could join us again."

Lia nodded with a smile. "Me too." She was also glad she'd forged a quick friendship with her co-worker. Alicia was a sweet person, and they had many things in common, including being separated from their mothers during childhood. Since Lia started working at the mobile vet clinic, Alicia always managed to brighten her day.

Alicia tilted her head, studying Lia with curious eyes. "Did you change your hair?"

Lia shook her head, puzzled. "I don't think so. Why?"

"It looks like you added streaks to it."

She gasped and lifted a small section of hair to inspect it. Sure enough, parts of it were stained in faint shades of blue and green. "Oh my! I don't know how many times I washed it to get the colors out of it. Zach and I played paintball last night." She turned to her nana with wide eyes. "Did you notice my hair?"

Nana pursed her lips like she was trying not to laugh and nodded. "Maybe a little on the way here, but I didn't think it would be helpful to mention it. It's barely noticeable. I like it, actually."

Lia scoffed and turned back to Alicia whose mouth quivered, but she reined in the developing giggle before speaking again. "I was so tired last night when Zach came to pick up Violet, I didn't even realize you all had played paintball." She released a weary sigh. "Violet kept me and Jace on our toes all evening."

"I'll bet she did." Lia released a half-hearted laugh while continuing to inspect her wild hair.

"She's sweet though, and such a blessing," Alicia continued.

Lia nodded in agreement but couldn't help being distracted by her colorful locks.

Alicia took notice and put her hand over Lia's. "Don't worry about your hair too much. It's very faint. I'm sure most people didn't even notice...and those who did probably think you're trying some hip new style."

"That's right," Nana chipped in, patting Lia's hand.

Lia let out a low groan before deciding to laugh it off. "Guess there's no point leaving now. Everyone's probably already seen it anyway."

"Yep, just own it now, girl." Alicia gave her a playful wink, lightening the mood.

"You're right. I should." Lia sat a little straighter, taking her friend's words to heart.

A few seconds later, Alicia's husband, Jace took his place on stage and began tuning his guitar. It turned out he'd recently become the lead song leader after the original one retired from the position. Lia smiled seeing Jace's service dog on the stage with him. Alicia had explained last Sunday, Jace no longer had seizures and didn't require the dog to be with him twenty-four seven anymore, but the congregation thought of Cooper as part of their church family and insisted he continued coming to church—kind of like a mascot of sorts. Plus, being a working dog his whole life, Cooper became bored without having a job, so he still accompanied Jace everywhere he went. Retired or not, they remained best friends.

Lia sang along with the words on the screen as Jace led the congregation in some hymns and contemporary songs. She didn't know all of the songs but tried her best to follow along. About two songs in, Lia heard Alicia greet someone and turned as Zach sidestepped into their row, holding a sleeping Violet.

"Here, you can sit by Lia," Alicia offered, just loud enough to hear over the music. Lia gave her a look and mouthed "thanks a lot", but her friend just winked. How had she forgotten Zach went to the same church as Nana?

"Sorry we're late," Zach said into her ear. "I slept in, and Violet waited to fall asleep until I picked her up last night. It's hard helping a sleepy four-year-old get ready for church."

"I bet she's not used to staying up so late." He nodded in response, and Lia offered him a warm smile, trying to extinguish the heat flaming up her cheeks. Her eyes darted from left to right, trying to see if anyone had noticed Zach taking his place next to her. It was true, their relationship was new and exciting. She looked forward to what the future could hold, but she didn't necessarily want to announce they were a couple yet. The older church ladies meant well, but they could unintentionally be nosey little matchmakers at times. Lia wasn't ready to explain what she and Zach meant to each other yet—not when she still wasn't certain yet herself.

She tried to pay attention and avoid looking at him, but that was impossible, not with his cologne drawing her in. When Lia finally did look up, she had to stifle a laugh. Zach's hair was streaked with a faint mosaic of colors too. Somehow it made her admiration of him grow even more. After all, it took a very brave and devoted man to show up at church with tie-dyed hair.

14

"Sorry about the stained hair fiasco," Zach said, leaning close to Lia's ear when the service ended. "I've been paintballing dozens of times, and that's never happened before."

She offered a shy smile and tucked a few strands of green tinted hair behind her ear. "That's all right. It's not a big deal."

"I wonder if the paintball place bought a different brand of ammunition this time. I didn't realize it until now, but the colors did seem more vibrant than usual."

"No problem, really. It will wash out eventually." Lia laughed, but it sounded forced. He had a suspicion she wasn't keen on having streaked hair. Hopefully the mishap wouldn't affect their relationship moving forward. To be honest, he really liked Lia. Her vibrant and slightly witty personality, her talent for photography, and her open-minded attitude were some of the qualities he enjoyed so far. Plus, she had a natural connection with Violet from the start and his little girl adored her.

Luna leaned forward to talk to him. "So glad you came today. What are your plans for after church?"

Zach grinned. "Actually, I had planned on coming to Hopper

Ear Cove for a little bit. Jace and Alicia invited us for lunch so we can talk more about the community garden afterward."

"You and Lia are invited, too," Alicia added from the other end of the pew.

"Oh, thank you. We'd love to." Luna grinned, but he noticed Lia's face paled. What had changed since last night? Was it just the stained hair or something else? Maybe after lunch they could take a walk alone to get to the bottom of it.

It wasn't that Lia didn't want to have lunch with Zach present. She just needed a good nap and time to file through her cluttered thoughts. However, after a strong cup of coffee at Alicia and Jace's apartment, she started feeling more like herself. It was crowded in their small kitchen, so after lunch, she took her dessert of cherry cheese pie out to the front porch where Zach was busy watching Violet play tug of war with Cooper.

"Looks like fun," she commented while sitting beside him on the step.

Zach nodded with a chuckle. "According to Alicia, Violet became best friends with him last night. Now they're inseparable. Colby's going to be so jealous when we come home."

"I bet." Lia absent-mindedly rolled the cherries off of her dessert and sampled a bite of what remained. The tangy sweetness rolled over her tongue, and she closed her eyes, savoring it.

"You don't like cherries?"

Lia swallowed and peeked over at him. "This might sound strange. Promise not to judge?"

A boyish grin crept over his face. "Cross my heart."

Satisfied and amused by his usual light hearted ways, she continued. "I love the taste of cherries, but I don't like the skin. Same thing with blueberries. I like them, but pureed into a smoothie or something like that."

He nodded. "I understand. Violet doesn't like cherries either. Something about the texture."

"Yeah, that's a good way to explain it. The texture just isn't right." She chuckled to herself. "Glad I'm not the only one who's picky about textures. I can't hardly eat yogurt if it has little chunks of fruit mixed into it either."

"Now that *is* weird." Zach arched an eyebrow at her. "Just joking."

Lia punched his shoulder playfully. "You better be."

He rubbed his shoulder, pretending to be injured. "No need for violence now."

Lia ignored him, but her mouth curved into a grin while returning her attention to Violet and Cooper. "You know, she has a natural way with animals like you do."

"Thank you."

"You're welcome. I admire what you all do...rescuing animals and all."

He shrugged. "In the beginning, I never thought we'd have so many, but I guess everything happens for a reason."

Lia nodded. "I didn't use to believe stuff like that, but now I'm starting to."

"What changed?"

She took in her surroundings with the blue sky and the path leading past the apartments. When she walked down to the stairway by the cliffs, there was a surround sound and view of the ocean. Lia didn't know why, but it calmed her restless heart. "I came here to help Nana, but I was also trying to escape real life. I'd just lost my job and was about to lose my apartment. The situation left me feeling very bitter. Nana helped me work through some things, though. I still can't believe I came here to help her, but in reality, she's done most of the helping. She gives such great advice."

He nodded. "I'd have to agree with you. I've had questions

about raising Violet before and Luna always knew just how to help."

"I'm glad to hear she's as much of a blessing in your life as she is in mine."

"Yep, she's been a Godsend."

"Lia, Lia!" Violet called. "Look, I taught Cooper a trick!"

She grinned at the little girl. "Awesome. Let me see."

"Cooper, dance," she commanded while spinning in a circle. The dog copied her movement, and Violet clapped in delight. "Good boy."

Lia and Zach applauded their performance. "Wow! Great job," she said. "I think you both have a career in theater.

Violet finished with a bow, and to Lia's amazement, Cooper followed suit. "She really has a way with animals, doesn't she?"

Zach nodded. "She's always been that way. It just seems to come naturally, like she speaks their language or something."

Lia finished her dessert while watching Violet and Cooper play. The little girl's carefree ways brightened her mood, serving as a reminder to be joyful and appreciate the simple things in life.

"It's such a nice day. You young folks should take a nice walk to the lookout," Nana offered a few minutes later when she came out on the porch with Alicia and Jace close behind. "It's my turn to watch Violet and Cooper's Broadway performance." She aimed a wink at Lia.

Zach stood and rubbed his stomach. "Think I need to walk off some calories after eating too much of that delicious pie."

Lia chuckled at his comment, noting his muscular build. "Like you need to watch your calories. A walk does sound good though. I'd love to see the progress on the house."

Alicia's face lit up with joy. "Wonderful! I can't wait to show you everything."

A few minutes later, they were on their way up the path to the cliffs. Lia was glad Nana had been nice enough to offer to watch Violet. Zach was a wonderful and devoted dad, but he needed some time for adult conversation, too. Reaching the halfway point, the guys branched off to take another look at the site for the gardens, leaving Alicia and Lia to themselves for a few minutes.

Alicia nudged her arm and spoke soft enough so the guys couldn't hear. "I want to hear more about this date."

Lia grinned, finally recovered from the multicolor hair incident. She waited until Zach moved a little further before responding. "It was fun. We went to this neat seafood place, and I'd never been paintballing before. Have you?" she asked, hoping the question would distract Alicia from asking more personal questions.

Alicia shook her head, cringing. "No, I've always been afraid it would hurt."

"It wasn't that bad, except when one hit my exposed knuckles. Kind of stung." She chuckled softly. "Zach's mask fogged up during the middle of our battle. I didn't realize he needed a timeout and accidentally got him right in the earlobe."

"Oh dear. I bet that didn't feel very good."

"Yeah, I felt so bad! But he was a good sport about it. I've dated guys who would get so mad about an accident like that." Lia bit her lip, realizing she'd unintentionally let the subject breeze right back to her and Zach, like stray leaves scattering across a yard.

"He seems like such a good guy. No wonder all the single ladies are drawn to him like a magnet."

Lia's brow arched like it had been snagged by a fishhook. "They are?"

Alicia nodded with a sheepish grin. "I probably shouldn't have said anything...but didn't you notice the group of them surrounding him as we left church?"

"Well...not *just* single girls," she attempted to argue. "There was that elderly lady who'd baked him a casserole to take home."

Her friend scoffed playfully. "Yeah, so she'd have the opportunity to tell him about her single granddaughter."

Lia shook her head. "Guess he's one of the most eligible bachelors on the islands, huh?"

"Well, not anymore, right? Now that he's dating you?"

She attempted to hide the heat rising to her cheeks in vain. "It was only one date. I don't know if that is enough to earn the title 'dating' really." She used her fingers to write imaginary quotations in the air.

Alicia frowned. "I'm sorry, Lia. I hope I wasn't being too pushy. I didn't mean to make you uncomfortable."

She managed a lopsided smile, although hiding her head in a rabbit den sounded like a more welcoming option. Didn't the locals call the island Hopper? If so, where were all the stinkin' rabbits anyway? "There's no need to apologize," she finally said, attempting to stay calm. "You were just curious about the date. All this drama is my fault. I'm battling the same insecurities as always. I over analyze and mess things up."

"Here, let's sit for a minute." Alicia led them to a lookout, and they both settled onto the edge of the cliff, letting their feet dangle over the edge. Lia couldn't deny it was a stunning view of the cove, with the afternoon sun making the water glow like liquid crystals. After a few moments of silence, Alicia touched her shoulder, offering a knowing expression. "As far as insecurities and over analyzing things go, I could have made myself a career out of that when I first moved here."

"Really?"

Her friend nodded. "Oh yeah. I was my own worst enemy, but Jace was patient. He didn't push me to talk about my past until I was ready. I guess I just want everyone to find that kind of love. That's why I was so excited to hear you were going on a date with Zach. You're both my friends, and I felt like you'd be well-matched. Can I ask you a question?"

"Sure." Lia gulped in preparation.

"Does the fact Zach is a single dad play a factor in your insecurities?"

She gazed at the horizon, watching the gulls hovering on the updraft, thinking over the question before turning back to Alicia. "To be honest...surprisingly, no. Violet is a wonderful little girl. She's so sweet and fun. The fact that Zach and Violet are a two for one deal really doesn't bother me."

"So, what *does* bother you?"

Lia sighed, taking a moment to think. If only her true feelings weren't as unpredictable as Georgia weather during hurricane season. "I guess Zach and I are too compatible. He's got that old-fashion charm, and I love it. But it leaves me feeling inadequate somehow, since I've always been the one in the relationship to put more into it, while the guy barely contributes. Maybe I'm waiting for something to go south, because...well my relationships always do eventually."

"I understand how past failed relationships can cause doubt to fester in your mind. I had one from high school that haunted me for years. But like the pastor's sermon today, I know now. All our trials have a purpose. I only recently healed from what happened. It took a lot of prayer and working through it. Plus, Jace..." Alicia smiled. "It's amazing how one *good* guy can make the bad ones fade into the past where they belong. I guess what I'm trying to say is, don't let the fear of another failed relationship make you miss out on something really amazing with Zach."

"You're right. I definitely don't want that." She turned to watch Zach talking and laughing while walking toward them. "I'll have to find a way to talk with him about how I'm feeling soon."

$\mathcal{Z}$ ach couldn't seem to figure women out. He'd thought the date with Lia had been enjoyable for both of them, but now she was sending him mixed signals. At church, she'd pretty much ignored him. She recovered and was almost her normal self after lunch, but now she was quiet as a mouse. He tried to put his concerns on the back burner and listen to Jace as he showed them the house.

"We're hoping to have the house completed by next year, if all goes as planned, but as you can see, there's still a lot to do." Jace motioned toward the Victorian style home with a wrap-around porch. It had scaffolding set up around the upper level, and he could see replacement siding on about one third of the structure, but the other two-thirds was stripped to the bare bones.

"Looks great so far."

"Thanks." Jace wrapped his arms around his new wife, Alicia while studying the house. "We weren't sure if this house would still be standing after Hurricane Arley hit. It was already in bad shape before the storm."

"But it looks like God meant for it to keep standing," Alicia added with a smile of contentment. "Now we're working on it little by little as our budget allows. Next week, a crew is coming to replace the roof."

"I can't wait to see the finished project," Lia said, finally breaking her silence. "I'm sure it will be lovely."

Zach listened as the newlyweds continued the tour of the house and grounds of the lookout. Last, they showed them the site of the old lighthouse. Jace informed them, it had been torn down because of its dilapidated condition, but after the house was done, they planned to rebuild it.

Afterward, Jace and Alicia headed back toward the apartments. Zach followed, but Lia touched his arm, stopping him. "Could I talk to you alone for a few minutes?"

"Sure." Zach's heart tumbled around in his chest like an off-balance washing machine. He hadn't been able to read Lia's strange behavior all day, and he had a feeling she was about to reveal everything all at once now. After letting Jace know they'd be down in a few minutes, he walked with Lia to the site of the old lighthouse.

She gave him a shy smile as the afternoon sun highlighted the green accents of her deep brown eyes. While speaking, she dropped her gaze to the rocky ground. "Before I start, I wanted to apologize for acting strange today. It has nothing to do with you. I had a wonderful time last night, but…"

Zach's heart lurched at her pause. It was the royal brush off he'd heard from a few girlfriends before Violet came into his life. 'I had a wonderful time and you're such a nice guy, but… we're too different.' or something similar. Zach didn't know what it was. Maybe he was too old-fashioned, or he talked too much, or any number of things that could turn a woman off. He should have kissed her last night. That would have proven the spark between them. Or maybe the fact he was a single dad scared her off. Zach thought it would be different with Lia, but like usual he'd been mistaken. It was disappointing since he liked Lia so much, but at least it would happen early on and not later, causing more heartache for both of them. "It's not going to work out," he finished for her. "It's all right. I understand."

Lia looked up at him again, blinking hard. "That's not what I was going to say at all."

"Really?" All his disappointment and regret fizzled into confusion. "Then what are you trying to tell me?"

"Only that I've been battling my own insecurities. You're different from any guy I've ever dated."

"Shockingly handsome?" Zach cut in to lighten the mood.

She laughed at his well-timed joke. "That and...well, to be honest, you're a good guy. After being a magnet for the bad ones, I don't really know how to act."

Zach put his hands in his pockets and raised an eyebrow. "I do have plenty of faults you may not have noticed yet. How do you know I'm such a good guy?"

She scoffed, shaking her head. "Believe me, I've been around enough rotten ones to recognize a good one."

He scratched his head, trying to understand, but that was harder than unscrambling some eggs. "So, I'm too good? Is that what's wrong?"

"No, nothing is wrong. It's perfect, and that's the part that scares me." She stifled a nervous laugh by biting her lip. "Am I making any sense at all? Or do you think I sound completely insane?"

"What I think is..." He moved closer to cup her cheek in his palm. "Somehow, we ended up on different pages, but I'm not going to stop reading the book until I've heard the whole story, okay?"

She nodded, and a tear dripped down her cheek. "With everyone else, I always prepared my heart, knowing the relationship would crash and burn eventually. But with you, the risk of my heart being broken if things don't work out is much higher."

He smiled and wiped away the tear with his thumb. "Why is that?"

Lia choked out a laugh. "Well, in case you haven't noticed, I like you a lot, Zach Nolan."

"I like you, too. I can't predict the future, but I promise you to do everything in my power to protect your heart. Loving always comes with a risk, but I'm willing to take that risk if it means we could have a future together. Are you?"

She nodded as more tears cascaded down her cheeks, but this time they were tears of joy. "Yes, I am."

Zach released a relieved sigh while wrapping his free arm around Lia's waist to draw her into his embrace. "I'm so glad to hear you say that." With Lia's head tucked under his chin and her arms wrapped around him, he closed his eyes, savoring the moment. Everything felt right, like they were always meant to hold each other.

A few seconds later, Lia peeked up at him, grinning. "After a speech like that I kind of expected…" She let out a giggle.

"What?"

Lia sighed. "Never mind." She gripped his collar, pulling him in for a passionate kiss.

When their lips parted again, Zach chuckled to himself, brushing a finger over her soft cheek. "Sorry, guess I'm out of practice." He pulled her closer, and she relaxed in his embrace as their lips met a second time. His regrets about neglecting to kiss her last night flew away. It wasn't meant to happen then. Their first kiss was destined to be here and now, where they both knew what they desired—a long-term commitment.

"Someone looks happy today," Kendall commented as she returned to the clinic after a walk with Zoe. She'd caught Lia and Alicia dancing to the radio while putting away some new supplies from a shipment from the mainland.

"Oh, it's nothing," she lied. Lia attempted to hide her blushing cheeks by leaning over to rub the Australian Shepherd's belly.

"No, it's certainly not nothing," Alicia blabbed from across the room. "He kissed her!"

Kendall's eyes lit up. "He did? Wow, Lia. That's awesome. I was hoping things would work out between you and Zach. He's such a nice guy."

She nodded, still battling the heat flaming in her cheeks. "Yes, he is." Lia grinned, finally deciding it was no use trying to hide her joy. It was hard to believe not so long ago, she'd been jealous, thinking Kendall was dating Zach. How wrong she'd been, but now she realized it stemmed from some truth. She'd been attracted to him from the beginning. In truth, their relationship was still so new and exciting, part of Lia wanted to shout it from the rooftops, while the other half wanted to keep the happy news all to herself. Living on a small island chain, she knew privacy was hard to come by. People at the Merriweather church had witnessed her sitting next to Zach, looking like a couple. She had no doubt word would spread like a flood. But should she care so much, now that she and Zach had worked so many things out yesterday? Lia concluded it was something she'd have to adjust to.

They were almost finished putting the new supplies away when Kendall's cell rang. A few seconds after answering it, her face turned white as the flesh of a coconut. She plugged one ear and headed for the door. "Hold on a sec, Tiff. I can hardly hear you. What happened?" Her voice trailed away as the RV door closed behind her.

Alicia exchanged a worried glance with Lia. "Well, that didn't sound very good."

"No, not at all."

16

*M*issing. The words evoked a terror in Kendall's heart, so much her hands tremored as she drove to Tiff's house. She didn't know the details but hearing the hopeless tone in Tiff's voice was enough to send Kendall's heart into a tailspin.

As it started raining outside, Kendall tapped on the steering wheel with her thumb, wishing the drive from Hopper to Merriweather could be shorter. Her foot continued pushing harder on the gas, sending her flying down the winding island roads at ten miles over the speed limit. Zoe whined from the passenger seat, prompting Kendall to slow down. There was no point in risking her life or someone else's. That wouldn't help Tyler. Besides, Alicia had been kind enough to lend her car for the afternoon and watch over the clinic. Wrecking Alicia's vehicle wouldn't be a very nice way of thanking her.

Still, the more Kendall tried to stay calm, the more panic seized her. Three weeks. He was scheduled to be home in *three* weeks. Why now? What was God doing? Kendall continued driving as the rain grew heavier and an ocean of confused thoughts washed over her like a tsunami wave. Driving past Banner General made matters worse—evoking memories of running into Tyler there before they were dating. He'd been helping Tiff stock the shelves, but Kendall wasn't expecting to see him. For the first month after she moved to Merriweather, he always seemed to be around, bugging her with his presence, making her absent minded. That time she fumbled for the groceries because his blue eyes distracted her. It wasn't until later when Kendall finally realized what a gem the Lord had sent her. If only he were here to bug her now—to hold her in his arms and never let her go.

"God please..." she whispered as rain splattered on the windshield, but the words wouldn't come. They remained lodged in her throat, choking her. Her mind betrayed her, picturing Tyler injured and helpless in some trench with no one to help him. Kendall started to hyperventilate. Tears clouded her eyes, and she heard the loud blaring of a horn. She swerved, just in time to miss a car coming from the other direction.

Shaking and crying, Kendall pulled off the road. Zoe whined and started licking her hand. She patted the dog, sniffling. "Sorry girl. I guess I really shouldn't be driving like this." She rested her head on the steering wheel and sobbed even harder. "God please..." The words still wouldn't come, but this time she thought of a verse from Romans 8:26 about the Holy Spirit interceding with groans too deep for words. If ever she needed the Holy Spirit to intercede for her, it was now. She closed her eyes and allowed Him to work. An image of Tyler appeared in her mind. He was surrounded by enemies on all sides. The image scared her until something else came into focus. The army of God surrounded him, protecting him from harm. Yes, that was what her heart desired—for her Marine to be safe—for him to return home to her.

Soon her cries dried up, along with the rainstorm outside. Kendall wiped her face on her sleeve and tried to steer the car back onto the road. The right tires protested, spinning in the wet sand. Kendall sighed and put her head against the back of the seat for a moment, closing her eyes. It was tempting to dissolve into tears again, but she fought against it. "Well, I guess a walk will be good for us anyway, huh girl?"

Zoe's tail thumped, and Kendall hooked up her leash. They stepped out of the car for the mile-long trek to Tiff's house. She'd call Alicia on the way and let her know about the situation. Since Jace was seizure free and able to drive now, he could take their truck and pull the car out of the ditch when he had a free moment. Kendall felt horrible about leaving the car on the side of the road, but right now, it was her only choice. Tiff, usually so calm and full of unshakable faith, had sounded so distraught on the phone. Kendall didn't want to keep her waiting any longer, and honestly, she needed Tiff just as much as she needed her. Even though they weren't technically sisters-in-law yet, she felt like family.

As Kendall walked with Zoe, her eyes were drawn to a double rainbow stretching across the sky. An unearthly calm fell over her, and she smiled through her tears. It felt like a promise God was taking care of things. He was watching out for Tyler, even when things were dark. After calling Alicia about her car, she worked up to a jog, making it to Tiff's house in a little over ten minutes. Her friend came out to the driveway when she arrived, and they sobbed in each other's arms.

"They can't tell me much," Tiff managed after a few minutes. "He was involved in a special op, and only half his squadron returned. I'm supposed to receive more information as they receive it." Tiff looked up. She wiped her eyes and looked around. "Did you jog all the way here?"

Kendall shook her head with tears still rolling down her cheeks and a grin tugging on her lips. "No, but that's a long story...involving sand, the bane of my existence as always."

Tiff laughed through her tears. "Some things never change. I'm glad you're here. I needed a good laugh."

"Me too." She studied Tiff's face, etched with worry, but now with a hint of relief. "It's going to be all right. God is going to protect him. I feel it in my heart."

Tiff nodded, her lips trembling. She motioned toward the house. "Let's head inside. We have a lot to talk about."

"Why are you having a sleep over on a school night?" Katie asked from across the table at dinner. Tiff's oldest daughter eyed her with both curiosity and a hint of suspicion. She was eight now, and smart as a whip. It wouldn't be long before the girl would discover the truth about her uncle.

Kendall exchanged a brief glance with Tiff before offering a brief explanation that would hopefully buy enough time for the girl's mother to work out how to tell her the whole truth about Tyler. "I took a few days off and thought it would be nice to spend that time with your mom. We're going to look through some old photos and scan them into the computer to make a nice surprise for Uncle Tyler when he comes home in a few weeks."

"Maybe we could help!" five-year-old Amy offered.

"I'd love that. Doesn't that sound fun, Katie?"

"Sure." The older girl nodded, but quickly returned her attention back to the lasagna on her plate.

Kendall knew the story about making a surprise for Tyler didn't satisfy her, but it would have to do for now. In truth, she'd decided to spend the night at Tiff's that night, both so she could be close if the military called with more information, and to help with the kids. Tiff was still strong as usual, but Tyler's missing status had hit her hard, reminding her of when her husband, Will, died overseas two years ago. Right now, she needed all the support she could get, so Kendall gathered a few essentials from home, and decided to stay for at least one night.

After dinner, she helped the kids with homework and played a few games with them. When it was time for bed, Kendall walked into Katie's room to say goodnight. The girl was still solemn as when they had eaten dinner. "What's wrong, sweetheart?" she asked while tucking her in.

"I know something happened to Uncle Tyler. Mommy doesn't want to tell me because she thinks I'm still a little kid."

Kendall sighed while sitting on the edge of the bed. "She doesn't think that. She knows you're growing up, just like I do. It's just..." she paused, praying for the right words that would inform, but not frighten the little girl. "Sometimes, it's hard to explain something, when we haven't quite figured it out how to feel ourselves. Your mom just needs some time. Then she'll tell you. I'm sure of it."

"I thought adults understood everything."

Kendall shook her head, offering a gentle smile. "Some things are easier to understand than others."

Katie crossed her arms with a frown. "Aunt Kendall, please tell me."

She swallowed a lump in her throat and smoothed the blanket. It was so sweet Katie already thought of her as an aunt. She wanted the truth and trusted Kendall enough to ask for it. She couldn't keep it in any longer. "All right, but you have to promise not to tell Amy or Micah. Your mom would explain it best so they won't worry, okay?"

Katie nodded. "I promise."

Kendall took a deep breath and prepared herself before speaking. "Uncle Tyler went on a special mission with his squadron. They were supposed to rescue some people who needed help. That sounds a lot like him, doesn't it? Going to help people?"

Katie nodded while swiping away a tear with her pajama

sleeve. "Did he get shot like Daddy did?"

Kendall shook her head. "I don't think so, but I can't be sure what happened. No one has heard from him in a few days." The little girl's chin trembled, so she took her hand. "It could mean anything. Uncle Tyler could be hiding somewhere or be helping keep people safe."

"Couldn't they just call him? Or use a radio to talk to him?"

"It's not that easy out where he is. He might be in a place where phones don't work. His radio could be broken. He'll probably come back to base soon."

Violet nodded, wiping away more tears. "What if he doesn't?"

"We can't think like that. Did you know prayer and faith are powerful things?"

She hugged her stuffed animal chipmunk tighter. "Uncle Tyler told me that before."

"Well, he's right. We just have to keep our faith and keep praying." She looked down at the chipmunk. "This was from Uncle Tyler, wasn't it?"

She nodded with a grin. "He always calls me chipmunk."

Kendall smiled, glad Katie had such a close relationship with Tyler. He'd been a father figure to his nieces and nephew since their father died. Now it was Kendall's turn to be an aunt for them. "How about every time you worry about Uncle Tyler, hug the chipmunk like you're hugging him? Then say a prayer for him. Do you believe God listens to our prayers?"

"Yes."

"Good, because He really does. He hears and answers, too. We can send a care package all the way from here to Uncle Tyler in the Middle East. God will take that hug and prayer and send it for us."

Katie grinned. "Really?"

Kendall nodded, feeling comforted herself. "Yes, because all things are possible through God. Do you want to send your hug and prayer right now?"

Katie nodded, and they prayed together. When they were finished, the little girl gave her a bear hug. "Thank you, Aunt Kendall. I feel better now."

"Me too, chipmunk. Me too."

After Katie settled in to sleep for the night, Kendall closed the door most of the way, leaving it open a small crack. She leaned against the wall for a moment to regain her composure. There was nothing quite like the prayer of a child. They spoke to the Lord with such a pure and sincere heart. She hoped Katie's prayer would be answered with a yes, and He would send Tyler safely home.

After making her way back downstairs, she crossed into the kitchen first, grabbing a tub of chocolate chip cookie dough ice cream from the freezer. Before dinner, she'd made a quick dash to her house down the street to gather some essentials for the night. She'd also grabbed the tub of ice cream, figuring it would be the perfect comfort food to share with her friend.

Kendall scooped some into two bowls and came into the living room, offering one to Tiff who sat on the couch watching the news. "Thought you might need some of this tonight."

Tiff broke her attention from the screen and aimed a hungry glance at the rich ice cream. "How do you know me so well?"

Kendall shrugged and sat next to her with her own bowl. "You're a lot like me, I guess. Plus, you know what they say. A bowl of ice cream a day keeps the doctor away."

Tiff laughed so hard she choked on her ice cream. "Don't think you remember that quote right." She grimaced and held her forehead. "Oh! Brain freeze."

She laughed and apologized to Tiff. "Okay, maybe that's not true, but ice cream does help me de-stress."

Tiff nodded, while getting another spoonful of ice cream—a smaller portion this time. "I can't argue with that." After eating it, she turned back to her. "Thank you for your help tonight. It makes it easier, just having you here."

"You're welcome."

Tiff furrowed her brow. "How was Katie?"

"She's doing all right, but I had to tell her what is going on. You know how perceptive she is." Kendall stirred her ice cream, hoping Tiff wouldn't be upset with her.

"I figured you did. I'm relieved really. I couldn't seem to keep my thoughts unscrambled tonight. I don't think she would have slept well tonight without some kind of explanation."

"Yeah, I can understand. I'm the same way. If I know something's not right, I think about it all night and fret."

A story about missing American soldiers came on the news station and Kendall held her breath. She listened, closely, hoping they had some new information to report, but it was mostly the same things they'd been hearing all day, and some speculation indicating they could have been captured. After a few minutes, Tiff shut off the TV and shook her head. "Sorry, I just can't listen to it anymore."

Kendall shrugged, looking down at her melting ice cream. "It's all right. I was getting tired of it, too. If anything new is discovered, they'll call us."

Tiff nodded and picked up the remote again. "Want to stream a movie?"

She grinned. "Ooo or maybe a musical?"

"*Grease?*"

"Exactly what I was thinking!"

They laughed and Tiff found it on the TV. Kendall leaned back on the couch and used a pillow to support her head. Coming to Tiff's had been a good decision. She re-thought her earlier joke about ice cream. What she should have said was, the company of a good friend every day keeps the worries away.

Kendall smiled to herself, watching John Travolta and Olivia Newton-John appear on the screen. It certainly was a blessing to have Tiff as a neighbor, friend…and one day, she hoped, a sister-in-law. She'd cling to that hope with every fiber of her being. Somehow Tyler was coming home. Until then, it was her job to keep the faith.

17

*O*n Tuesday and Wednesday, Lia did her best to pick up the slack at the vet clinic. Usually, she just took care of greeting customers and kept track of the accounting side of things. However, with Kendall taking a few days off, she worked full-time. She helped Alicia feed the animals they were boarding in the RV or cleaning the kennels, among other various jobs. Lia had to move around her schedule a bit for her photography clients, but she didn't mind. It was an emergency situation, and Kendall had become a good friend. She wanted to support her as much as possible.

After talking with Kendall that morning, she discovered they still hadn't heard anything back about her boyfriend, Tyler, but she sounded hopeful. She planned on coming back to work tomorrow. Meanwhile, the pastor had been contacted and all the church members were praying for Tyler and the other Marines who were missing. On Sunday, after the main service, they were organizing a special time of prayer in support of Tyler's family and Kendall. Apparently, he was pretty well-known local hero around the island, and it was touching how the island residents came together to support each other.

For the first time, Lia pictured what life would be like if she remained on the Independence Islands. She loved how close-knit the community was, and her photography business seemed to be off to a good start. While she enjoyed working for Kendall, but maybe one day she could do photography full-time. Also, the thought of living close to Zach held an undeniable appeal. Unfortunately, she'd been so busy, they'd hardly had a chance to talk since Sunday, but that would change on the weekend. They had their kayaking date all planned out for Saturday, and Lia couldn't wait.

When their last client of the day left, Lia checked her phone for the time at gasped seeing it was fifteen after four. "I'm supposed to be at the Belshaw Mansion at four thirty to photograph Carly and Luc's cats!"

Alicia's eyes grew wide as saucers. "Well, you better go now. Their butler is a real stickler about late arrivals. Believe me. I showed up a few minutes late when it was time for their yearly shots, and it was like pulling teeth to convince him to let me in."

Lia groaned. "Oh no. This is going to be a train wreck. If I make a bad impression with the Belshaws, no one's going to want to hire me."

"Then what are you waiting for? Go! I'll finish up here."

Lia took a look around the clinic and scrunched her nose. "Are you sure? I'd hate to leave you alone with so much to clean up."

Alicia waved away her concern and smiled. "I'll be fine. Just go before you're late."

Lia gathered her things quickly and opened the door. "Thanks. I really owe you one."

"Thank you for offering to sponsor the gardens Mr. Belshaw. I think this is a project that will benefit many on the islands."

"Of course," Luc said from behind the desk in his office. "I'm happy to contribute to a good cause. Truly, I wish I'd thought of the brilliant idea myself. Oh, and please, call me Luc."

"Okay, well, thank you, Luc. Jace and I appreciate your support."

"Yes, I'm looking forward to it." Luc looked down at his phone. "Sorry I don't have more time to talk. My pilot will be here shortly."

"That's fine. I don't want to keep you."

"Carly and I would love it if you and Lia came over for dinner sometime."

He nodded. "That would be great. Thanks for inviting us."

They shook hands and Luc led the way out of the office. Once in the hall, they parted ways, with Luc walking to the left and his secretary leading Zach to the right and down the regal staircase toward the front entrance of the mansion. Zach tried not to gawk at all the fancy architecture, sculptures, and paintings on the way out, but it was impossible. They were everywhere. He felt like he'd stepped off the Independence Islands and been transported all the way to France.

He continued taking in all the sights while exiting the mansion and was so preoccupied, he didn't realize someone was approaching him.

"Zach?"

He looked straight ahead and blinked hard. When he realized who it was, a smile bloomed on his lips. "Bonjour, mademoiselle." He reached for Lia's hand and planted a kiss on the top of it. "I was so distracted by all the beautiful artwork...I didn't notice the most stunning piece of all."

She giggled, blushing to a lovely shade of pink. "I didn't know you spoke French, monsieur."

He gave her a playful wink. "Only a few phrases. I took French as an elective in college."

"That's neat. I took it in high school."

"So, what are you doing here?"

She grinned and held up her camera bag. "I'm supposed to meet with Carly and take pictures of her cats."

Right then, the butler who'd escorted him outside returned to greet Lia. "Are you, Mademoiselle Diaz?" His French accent was so thick, Zach could hardly understand him.

Lia nodded. "Yes, I was scheduled to meet Mrs. Belshaw at four-thirty."

"Madam Belshaw called to say she is running a little late. Would you prefer to wait in the sitting room, or if you would like, a tour of the gardens would be lovely this time of year."

Lia paused with a perplexed look. He guessed she was trying to decode the words through his thick accent as well. After a moment, her eyes lit up with understanding. "I'd love to see the gardens." She turned to him. "Do you want to come along too, Zach?"

"Sure." He nodded and then looked at his phone. "Oh, wait. I forgot I have to pick up Violet from a play date at five. I have a few minutes to spare though. How about I walk down there with you? Then I'll go."

She agreed, and they followed the butler down the path, bordered by tulips. During the walk, Zach took the opportunity to hold Lia's hand, savoring the way her soft palm fit into his. Seeing her today had been a pleasant and unexpected surprise after thinking he'd have to wait until Saturday when they'd have their date.

When they reached the gate leading to the garden, the butler opened it to let them in. His thick brows furrowed. "You may walk along the path, and sit on the benches, but please do not lay a finger on Monsieur Belshaw's plants. They are very delicate, *oui?*"

They agreed and Lia attempted to keep a straight face as the butler turned to go. When they couldn't see him anymore, she turned to him with a giggle. "I feel like we're second graders who've been given an ultimatum by a school principal."

He nodded, chuckling. "Yeah, me too. Guess he's just doing his job."

She agreed as they took a brief survey of the garden before sitting together on a bench toward the center of it, facing a fountain. Lia looked around in awe at the variety of budding plants in well landscaped beds. There were elegant arches overhead with blooming vines trailing all the way up. She'd never seen such a well-tended and majestic garden.

"I thought the garden I inherited was time consuming to tend. I can't imagine the maintenance involved in this one. I'm really kind of jealous of this garden, regardless of the upkeep. It's pretty amazing."

Lia nodded. "Yeah, I've heard many of Luc's paintings were inspired by this garden. It's kind of famous among the islanders. I'm sure the Belshaws have groundskeepers whose only jobs are to tend to this garden and keep it looking amazing twenty-four seven."

He shrugged "I guess you're right. Mine's the perfect size for what I can take care of. I would like to talk to Luc sometime about all the plants in here though. About a quarter of them are varieties I've never heard of."

"I'm sure he'd love to tell you all about them sometime. From what Kendall has said, he's a real down-to-earth kind of guy, even if he is a billionaire."

He nodded. "I could tell that today while talking to him. He's agreed to sponsor the community gardens on Hopper."

"That's wonderful! It's all coming together, isn't it?"

"Yep, we'll start construction soon and hopefully have some plants started by April." He checked his phone again before rising to a standing position. "Well, I hate to leave so quickly, but I really have to go pick up Violet."

She stood up to give him a goodbye hug, as an unexpected ache filled her heart. "It's going to be difficult waiting until Saturday to see you again." The words had slipped out before Lia could restrain herself. Was she really that smitten with Zach already?

"Guess we better make this moment count then." He leaned forward to kiss her, and she wrapped one arm around his neck. A moment later, he surprised Lia by dipping her backward for a kiss. Her heart pounded so loud, she feared it would explode. He certainly knew how to sweep a girl off her feet. He grinned after bringing her back up. "Sorry, I guess the French ambiance inspired me."

"Guess so," she managed, cheeks flaming.

He backed up, still sporting a boyish grin. "*Au revoir, mademoiselle.*"

"Yeah, um, see ya," she managed, biting her lip and wavering a little on her feet. He turned around and disappeared around the bend in the garden path. Lia waited until hearing the gate close before sitting back on the bench. "Wow," she said breathlessly, as a goofy grin spread across her face.

"Wow, is right!" a woman's voice said from behind her.

Lia jumped and stood up, but her shoulders relaxed a moment later when Carly appeared from the back entrance to the garden. She managed a nervous smile, her cheeks still burning. "You saw all that?"

Carly nodded with a guilty grin. "Sorry, I wasn't trying to spy, but when I came in, I saw you two were having a special moment and didn't want to interrupt. I'm glad to see this garden is still inspiring romance. He looks like quite a catch."

"Yep, he is." Lia laughed at Carly's boldness. She had a fun personality, and she thought they'd be quick friends with Kendall's younger sister. She hadn't known what to think of

Carly at first, since most rich people she met in the past acted snooty. However, her laid back personality made it obvious marrying into money hadn't changed her negatively.

"Sorry, I'm late," Carly said with a sigh. "I'm taking some art and business classes at the college. Pretty soon I hope to have my own mobile art studio, and I'm trying to hone my skills, you might say."

"That's a great idea. Kendall told me you're going to teach art lessons eventually. I would take one of your classes."

"Oh, thanks for saying that! You're so sweet." She sighed and adjusted the sunglasses resting on top of her head. "Well, I guess we better head inside and get the cats ready for their photo session. It's about feeding time, so it will be easier to get them into the room and they'll be more affectionate and ready to cooperate. Although, I'll make no promises about Descartes. He can be pretty moody."

Lia chuckled. "I've heard about him, but I'm up for a challenge."

"Good." Carly motioned for Kendall to follow. "Because this might get interesting."

Zach arrived back on his street, happy as a clam, but slightly embarrassed. What had gotten into him—dipping and kissing Lia like that? He remembered when he'd developed his first crush in middle school. His mom knew something had changed about him. "Oh, I see what's going on," she said at dinner. "You've been bitten by the love bug." Zach had been embarrassed at the time, but now the memory made him smile. It ended up being a short-lived romance, like most teenage relationships, but that wasn't important. It was the talk his mom had given him about dating. She told him not to settle for just anyone, and her advice had stuck with him. She said one day he'd be bitten by the love bug again, but to wait for the right girl —the girl God intended for him.

Now that Zach had met Lia, he thought she could be the one his mom talked about. She was not only beautiful, but smart, funny, and talented. Lia made him feel like a kid again—a kid with a crush for the first time. Everything was so new and exciting. But maybe it was more than a crush this time. Maybe he had been bitten by the love bug again, but this was the right girl, like his mom predicted.

Zach stopped by the neighbor's house and picked up Violet. She jabbered on and on about her playdate as he drove the short distance to their house and parked in the driveway. As he turned off the car, she stopped talking for a minute and looked out the window, pointing. "Daddy, who's that on the porch?"

He stared for a while and blinked hard, not believing his eyes. The young woman must have been there for a while because she had rested her head against the siding of the house and appeared to be sleeping. He hadn't seen her in years, but there was no mistaking her curly, sandy brown hair and her heart-shaped face. He gulped back his nerves and turned to look at his daughter. "Violet, you're about to meet your Aunt Emmy."

18

*Z*ach scrubbed the dishes in the sink a little too hard while trying to buy himself some time to think. Not that he didn't want to see Emmy. He loved her and prayed for her often. The dishes gave Zach a welcome distraction from the current situation bombarding him. He'd spent two years trying to get in contact with Emmy without any luck. He finally gave up, shifting his focus to Violet.

In the absence of a mother, she needed a responsible guardian who was attentive to her needs. Not a distracted uncle who was always contacting the authorities to see if Emmy had turned up in a rehab or in jail somewhere. Now his sister had returned. Part of his heart rejoiced while the other half tremored with uncertainty. What were her intentions? Was this a short visit, or did she intend to stay for a while? And what did this mean for Violet?

"You've turned into a pretty good cook," Emmy commented while taking a seat at the kitchen island. "I can't tell you how long it's been since I had meatloaf that didn't taste like cardboard."

He turned away from the sink briefly to smile at her. "I used Mom's recipe."

Emmy's expression turned solemn. "You kept her recipe book?"

"Yeah, it was one of the few things I took from the old house. I can make you copies of your favorites if you want. It always makes me feel closer to her when I make dinners she used to."

His sister's eyes took on a hollow look, like her soul had somehow disconnected from her body. "That's all right, Zach. I never have much time for cooking anyway. Up until last year, I was homeless in Miami. Then I moved into this women's shelter with better meals, but the people there always cooked for us. I've never really learned to cook for myself, except for stuff like mac and cheese or ramen."

Zach frowned. "Emmy, I wish you would have called me. You know I would have helped."

Emmy shrugged. "You have your own life to worry about... and Violet." She bit her lip and her eyes clouded over. "How has she been? Hearing her talk at dinner so well...it opened my eyes to how much I've missed in her life. I hadn't thought of how big she would be now."

He loaded a few of the plates he'd scrubbed into the dishwasher. "She's doing really well. Next year she'll be in kindergarten."

Emmy's eyes grew round as one of the serving bowls waiting to be washed. "Kindergarten? Wow, I didn't realize that was coming up so soon."

"Yep, I'm not quite prepared for it either. Violet will be fine though. She's smart as a whip and excited about being a 'big girl' as she calls it."

Emmy chuckled softly—her eyes glued to the fruit bowl resting on the island. "Thank you for taking care of her all these years. I...I never intended to be gone for this long, but I'm going to make up for that now."

Zach continued concentrating on the dishes, scared to ask what Emmy meant by that statement. Did it mean she intended to stay around the islands? Or something else. He was too mentally drained to get into that conversation tonight. He loaded the silverware, put soap into the dishwasher and started it before turning to face her. "Well, I'm sure you're tired. If you're ready, I'll show you the spare room with the futon. We'll talk more in the morning."

"Yeah, I'm beat," she agreed with a yawn and followed him upstairs.

After getting everything settled for Emmy, Zach crossed the hallway to Violet's room. Tired out from her playdate, she'd skipped dessert and gone to bed thirty minutes after dinnertime. He'd already tucked her in and read a bedtime story before coming back downstairs to do the dishes, but for some reason, he felt the urge to check on her a second time.

In the dim illumination from the night light, he watched her tiny form moving up and down at even patterns. Her curly hair was splayed over one side of the pillow and her heart-shaped face looked relaxed and peaceful. Her resemblance to Emmy was uncanny. His thoughts drifted to Emmy when they were children—before everything went wrong. So innocent, boisterous, and full of life. It was a shame life had been so cruel to Emmy—stealing her childhood and innocence like a thief. The last thing he wanted was for the same to happen to Violet.

It had been almost five years since Emmy showed up at his Savannah apartment with a little bundle in her arms. Violet had only been a few weeks old—so tiny, beautiful, and precious.

"I didn't have anywhere else to go," Emmy had told him. "Can we stay here…just until I get back on my feet?"

Zach had agreed in an instant. He could never turn his sister and young niece away. Over the several weeks that followed, Emmy left every morning, saying she had job interviews. Zach watched Violet for her or called a sitter if he had to work, hoping his support would help his sister find a stable job. However, when she returned, she often smelled of stale smoke or alcohol. Then, one day, he found a suspicious bag of pills in her drawer.

"They're only my prescription," she'd argued when he confronted her about it.

"Prescriptions come in bottles with your name on them, Emmy. They don't come in ziplocked bags. Where did you get them?"

"You're not in charge of me! I don't have to answer to you." Emmy stormed off to the spare bedroom.

The next morning, she was all smiles, acting like nothing had happened, but he refused to let the incident go, telling her it wasn't just her life she was risking, but her infant daughter's. Emmy argued Violet wasn't affected directly by her lifestyle because she drank formula, but he didn't accept that excuse. "There's a rehab close by that I think we should consider," he told her. "I'm not saying this to judge your lifestyle. I just want to help you."

"Stop trying to run my life. You're my brother, not my father."

"I'm not trying to act like that, but I can't just stand by while you keep making decisions that could hurt you or Violet."

The rest of the day, Emmy gave him the cold shoulder, and the next morning the house was deathly quiet. He walked to the spare bedroom, finding it completely empty except for the crib and Violet's things. The sudden cry from an infant revealed the sobering truth. He crossed to the crib in the corner, and with tears dripping down his face, lifted his sweet little niece out of the crib. "Looks like it's just you and me now, pumpkin. But don't worry. We're going to be all right."

A few minutes later, he'd found the letter from Emmy on the kitchen table. *You're right. My choices aren't good for Violet. I've tried to be a good mother, but I can't give her what she needs. I know you want to help me, but I'm not going back to rehab. Ever. I'll find the help I need in my own way. But for right now, my baby will be better off with you. Please tell Violet I love her. Emmy.*

Zach wiped a few tears as the memory faded. He continued watching Violet sleep, amazed at how much she'd grown since the day he became her guardian. After Emmy left, he'd debated with himself for months whether she should call him Uncle Zach or Daddy. As time passed, when it became clear his sister wasn't coming back, he chose the latter and moved to the Independence Islands, where he and Violet could have a fresh start. The world could be a cruel place, and the little girl already had to grow up without her mother. He at least wanted her to have a father and a normal childhood, without having to explain to other people why she was raised by an uncle instead of her real parents. As far as he was concerned, the first time Violet called him Dada as a baby, all his lingering reservations vanished. She was his daughter.

Zach's gaze drifted to the closed bedroom door across the hallway where his sister slept, and fear gripped his heart like a vice grip. While he loved Emmy with all his heart, he didn't trust her. Not that he wanted to keep Violet from her mother. In fact, Zach wanted Emmy to be a part of her life. However, given his sister's track record of drug use and running away, he didn't want Violet caught up in the whirlwind. Until he knew Emmy could be trusted and had her addiction under control, he couldn't leave them alone together. How would he sleep with so many questions about his daughter's safely swirling in his mind?

In an instant, he made the decision and gathered Violet into his arms, along with her favorite blanket and Henrietta, the stuffed chicken. He brought her to the downstairs bedroom and tucked her in with Henrietta. With Violet safe, he rested on the other side of his bed with a relieved sigh. Now he could sleep soundly.

His eyes had barely closed when he felt movement on the

bed. He opened them, seeing Violet had turned to face him. He saw the outline of her cute little face smiling at him. "I love you, Daddy," she whispered around a yawn.

Zach sat up halfway to kiss her forehead. He smiled, realizing even in the darkness she brought so much light into his life. "I love you too, pumpkin."

Friday morning at work, Lia grinned so wide her mouth hurt when Zach's number scrolled across her phone screen. Memories of their romantic kiss in the Belshaw Estate gardens raced through her thoughts as she clicked the talk button. Putting the phone to her ear, she spoke in a low voice since Kendall was treating a patient in the back room. "Bonjour, stranger. How are you?"

He only responded with "Hi," and the long pause following evoked worry in her heart.

"Is...everything all right?"

"Yeah, it's just...I hate to ask this, but would you mind if we postponed our date to next weekend? Something has come up."

Lia slumped into the office chair behind the desk and tried to keep her voice upbeat. She'd been dreaming about the date all week but knew Zach wouldn't postpone their date unless it was absolutely necessary. "Sure, that's fine, but what's up? Is Violet sick?"

"No, she's fine, but I'd like to talk to you in person. It would be hard to explain over the phone. Would you be able to come over after work?"

Lia opened her mouth to agree, before resting her head in her hand with a sigh. "I'm sorry, I just remembered I have two photography gigs that have already been rescheduled once because I had to work extra at the clinic."

"That's okay. Maybe Sunday after church? You could come over for lunch."

"Yeah, that would work." Lia responded in a bright tone but when the call disconnected, she felt like a heavy boulder had been laid on top of her chest. Zach's voice had sounded strained, like there was a tight string wound around his vocal cords. Something was definitely wrong, and it had to be serious since he wouldn't tell her over the phone. Lia's mind cluttered with possibilities, but none of the explanations she came up with seemed to fit. Her heart dropped in despair. All her relationships went south eventually, but she'd really hoped this one would stick. It turned out she was wrong again.

ach grinned as he set down a set of three aces. Afterward, he discarded his last card.

Emmy groaned, as she looked at the five cards still in her hand. "Wow, guess I'm a little rusty at Rummy."

"It's all right. You'll do better in the next round." He gathered the cards and started shuffling them. It was nice having the opportunity to spend time with his sister while Violet took an afternoon nap.

"Are you sure? If I remember right, you've always been a card shark."

"If you think I'm bad, you should play this game with Violet. She beats me all the time."

She arched an eyebrow. "She's not even five yet and knows how to play Rummy?"

He nodded with a hint of pride running through him. "Yeah, she's really good with numbers, and knows all her letters and sounds."

"You must have a lot of time to work with her."

"Working from home does have its benefits. I'm not sure

what I'm going to do next year when she starts kindergarten. I'm going to be bored out of my mind."

Emmy went silent as the grave while he dealt the cards again. When she finally looked up, the determination in her blue eyes sent chills up his spine. "I found a nice place in Miami. My boyfriend and I are going to split the rent. The unit is close to the playground, and the school is only a few blocks away. I think Violet would love it. We just need a little help on the deposit and first month's rent…"

Zach's brain whirled into overdrive. She wanted to take Violet? They would be hours away in another state? It was the worst-case scenario he could think of.

"So, what do you think?" His sister was asking. It was obvious to him now that she'd been talking the whole time, but he'd been too preoccupied to hear her. "Could you loan us the money? We'd pay you back. Axel just applied for the lead position at the carwash and I'm looking for a waitressing job."

Zach blinked hard, still dumbfounded. After a few seconds, the realization hit what she was asking. He leaned forward, knowing he needed to put his two cents in now, before things progressed. "I'd be happy to lend you money for an apartment if you need it, but I think you should live here for a while. That would give you time to get to know Violet. There are also waitressing jobs here. I just saw a wanted sign there last week at Granny's. It would also give you more time to build your savings."

Emmy scoffed and crossed her arms over her chest, her blue eyes flaming. "Zach, weren't you listening? My boyfriend lives in Miami. I can't stay here on this tiny boring island out in the middle of nowhere."

"And I can't allow you to uproot Violet like this."

Emmy's eyes flamed at him. "I'm her mother!"

His expression softened, trying to defuse the situation. "You're right. You are, but as her mother, you need to think about Violet's happiness above your own. She's lived here with me for most of her life and she doesn't know you yet. Kids need time to adjust...and they need stability."

She wrenched away from her chair and stood. "Oh, so now I'm unstable?"

He shook his head. "I never said that. I love you, Emmy, and I want what's best for you and Violet. You have good intentions, but a lot goes into raising children. It takes a lot of time and patience. Even with all the time I've spent with Violet I'm still learning this."

She let out a sardonic laugh. "I should have known this would happen. You've always tried to run my life. I'm not a little girl anymore, Zach. You can't tell me what to do!" With that, Emmy whipped around and dashed up the stairs.

Zach rested his head in his hands, praying for wisdom. Things couldn't have gone much worse. He heard the shower come on and hoped when Emmy came back out, she'd be willing to compromise. The last thing he wanted was for his sister to do something in anger, like find a lawyer.

"Daddy?"

Zach looked up and managed a smile for his daughter. "Hi pumpkin. Did you have a good nap?"

She rubbed the sleep out of her eyes and nodded while hugging Henrietta close. "Is Aunt Emmy mad at you? I heard her yelling."

"She's just having a bad day. We have those sometimes, don't we?"

She nodded. "Like last week when I spilled orange juice all over my drawing?"

"Yeah, that's a good example."

Violet tilted her head like a puppy. "Did you spill orange juice on something Aunt Emmy liked?"

Zach chuckled and pulled her into his lap, kissing her cheek. "Something like that."

The dog whined and pawed at the bell on the door.

"I think Colby needs to go outside. Do you want to walk with us? Then we can walk down the path to the beach and make a sand castle. Maybe I can find some more pearls for our collection, too."

Her eyes brightened. "Can I bring Henrietta?"

A genuine smile tugged at his mouth, proving again that Violet could bring a ray of light to any situation. "Sure, Henrietta is welcome. We'll just keep her away from the water, so she won't be swept away. I don't think chickens can swim."

"Plop!"

A choked gasp emitted from Lia's mouth as she peered over the edge of the ferry railing. A tiny flurry of bubbles was all the evidence remaining of her cellphone. "Well, that just happened." Lia groaned, resting her arms on the railing and lowering her head in disbelief and regret.

Her second photography gig had been postponed a second time by the clients this time. Taking advantage of the extra time, Lia hurried to the slip for the six o'clock ferry. With her schedule opened up, maybe she could salvage her meeting with Zach. Remembering how odd he'd sounded on the phone, Lia boarded the ferry, deciding to call him on the way to let him know she was coming after all.

Once parked on the ferry, she exited her car and moved toward the railing, retrieving her phone from her purse along the way. Right as she dialed, the horn sounded, causing her to jump and fumble with the phone. The device bounced off the railing, spiraled downward and was gobbled up by the hungry mouth of the sea. Lia imagined schools of fish at the bottom of the ocean floor scrolling through all her flowers and landscape photography. The young little fish students were probably getting bright ideas about living on dry land one day like the *Little Mermaid,* and now their fishy parents were totally going to blame her for putting the idea in their heads! She pictured the parents glaring at her from the ocean floor.

Lia shook away her crazy fantasy, although it was an amusing distraction. It was a coping mechanism she turned to when things in her life went haywire. Zach returned to her thoughts. She hoped her assumptions had been wrong and nothing was seriously wrong with him or Violet. As the ferry ride to Sparrow dragged on and on, Lia paced. After all, without her phone, she didn't know how else to distract herself.

Back on land ten minutes later, she was en route to Zach's house. The drive didn't take long, and as she walked up to knock on the door, her heart galloped in her chest. After ringing the doorbell, she waited, biting at her fingernails to keep herself occupied. When no one answered, she tried again.

This time, to her shock, a woman's voice called out. "Hold on, I'm coming, I'm coming. You people are so impatient these days!" Lia stepped back with wide eyes as the door opened. The woman wore a robe and had a large towel wrapped around her head. "Can I help you?" she asked, indignance radiating through her tone.

Lia glanced at the numbers on the side of the house to confirm she hadn't knocked on the wrong door. Sometimes anxiety caused her to do strange things, but no, it was the right house all right. "I...I'm sorry," she stuttered. "I just wasn't expecting..."

"So, what is it?" The woman asked, scoffing with impatience. "Are you from the post office with a delivery or something I can sign for?"

Lia shook her head. Something about the woman seemed familiar to her, but she couldn't put a finger on what it was. "No, I'm not delivering anything. I was actually here to talk to Zach. Is...is he here?"

The woman braced her hand on one hip, her eyes sparking at the mention of Zach. "No, he took my daughter for a walk. I have no idea where they went. You'll have to call him or come back later."

With that, the woman shut the door, leaving Lia standing outside, mind whirling with the shock. The words "my daughter" replayed over and over in her mind. Suddenly, she realized why the woman's distinct heart-shaped face and long lashes were familiar. She was the spitting image of Violet.

Tears stung Lia's eyes as she rushed back to her car and drove off as fast as the vehicle would allow. The situation was much worse than anything she could have imagined. Zach's ex was not only back in the picture. She was staying at his house and using his shower. Were they getting back together? Zach had said he wanted to talk in person about something, so that had to be the reason.

Lia wiped her tears as her shock and heartbreak morphed into anger. That was the last straw. She was done with men. Done with dating, period. She'd fallen for a good guy this time and look what had happened? No, from now on she'd stay single and take care of herself. Love just wasn't worth the effort.

20

*B*y Sunday morning at breakfast, Emmy had cooled down from their heated discussion on Friday. She came downstairs for breakfast in the morning, and at least greeted Violet with a smile. "Something smells good."

"Daddy made French toast."

"Mmm...my favorite."

Zach smiled as he walked to the table with their breakfast and set the plate on a hot pad. "I'm glad I remembered it right."

As they started eating, Violet perked up. "This afternoon, Lia's coming over. We're making fried chicken in the air fryer. She likes it that way cuz its healthier."

Emmy shrugged. "I like the grease. Doesn't seem like it would taste as good without it."

"Yeah, I thought that too at first, but it really tastes pretty good. We do spray it with a little olive oil, but it still ends up being healthier than the traditional method."

Emmy continued eating, not really showing much interest in their conversation anymore. It gave Zach an opportunity to check his phone. There was still no response from Lia, even though he'd sent her several messages yesterday. At least he'd see her later on at church. Maybe afterward, he would have a chance to explain the situation with Emmy. That reminded him of something, and he looked back at his sister. "We have church this morning. I'd really like it if you came with us."

Emmy recoiled. "Thanks, but I think I'll stay here. I haven't been to church in years."

"Now is the perfect time to start," he tried. "The people there are really nice."

She stared at her plate while cutting up a piece of French toast. "Maybe next time."

Zach was discouraged by her lack of interest, but he didn't push the matter any further. "Well, you can expect us back at around noon," he informed her before picking up his plate and taking it to the sink. He'd only eaten a few bites, but since Emmy had arrived, he hadn't had much of an appetite. The thought of Violet moving to another state tied his stomach in knots. If they couldn't come to an agreement, he worried Emmy would try to hire a lawyer to get what she wanted. Zach doubted the court would side with his sister, because there was evidence of abandonment and drug use on her record.

However, he wanted to avoid that route at all costs. He loved Emmy and wanted to re-create a healthy friendship with her, but he couldn't pretend to be okay with her taking Violet—at least without some kind of transitional period. Only time would tell if Emmy was trustworthy and had the skills to be a full-time mother, but her impatient, angry, and impulsive behavior wasn't instilling much confidence in him that she was ready.

Zach had never been more thankful to see Sunday arrive. He needed to be in the house of the Lord and with His people. Also, maybe he could confide in the pastor for advice. Not to mention, Lia would be there.

"I'm worried about you," Nana said as they sat in their pew at church. "You've been a nervous wreck since Friday night, didn't hardly eat anything yesterday, and you look so pale."

"I'm fine," Lia lied and concentrated on finding the verse listed in the bulletin on her Bible app. She'd decided there were a couple of good things about the time she'd spent on the islands—her renewed relationship with Jesus, spending time with her nana, and the new job opportunities. Besides that, all the charm of the islands had dissipated after finding out about Zach reconnecting with his ex. Lia had made a decision. She'd told Nana she'd stay with her for two months, and she had every intention of keeping that promise. There was a week and a half left until she'd upheld the agreement. Then she would move back to her apartment. If she advertised her photography business—maybe even created her own website for the business, she hoped it would take off. Also, there had to be more part-time secretary jobs she could look for to earn extra income. Now that she'd gotten the whole magazine job out of her head, her realm of opportunities had broadened. She would be fine back in the city.

The only part she dreaded was telling Nana. Lia thought deep down Nana probably hoped Lia would remain living on the islands. Until now, she'd been seriously considering the idea. However, now she just wanted to escape and never see Zach's face again. The part that made her heart ache most was the thought of not seeing Violet again. She was such a sweet girl and wouldn't understand.

She saw Kendall and Tiff wave at her before sitting near the front since they were having the special prayer service for Tyler after the main service. As everyone else started to filter into the sanctuary and take their seats, Lia tried to move her troubling thoughts to the back burner. She was at church to worship God. Not to fret over things she couldn't change.

"Should we save a seat for Zach and Violet?"

Lia shook her head and made up an excuse. "There are so many people here today in support of Tyler Banner, I'd hate to make it harder for them to find available seats. If he comes in late, he might want to stay near the back to not disrupt the service anyway."

Nana shrugged. "All right. I didn't think just two spots would make much of a difference, but we'll just leave the seats open for anyone if you want."

Later, two people scooted into the pew but sat on the far end. Maybe that would be enough for Zach to choose another seat. However, that thought was short-lived when he came in thirty seconds later. He stopped at her pew and smiled at her before squeezing past the people on the end to sit next to her.

She stood up like there was a spring attached to the seat. "I... I have to go."

Nana studied her with concerned eyes as she scooted out of her side of the pew, away from Zach. "What's wrong, dear?"

"I can't do this. I just can't."

She rushed out of the sanctuary as fast as her legs would carry her without running. Lia managed to keep her composure until bursting through the doors to the outside. Tears pricked her eyes as she walked down the sidewalk. She didn't know where she was going. It was just necessary to get away. How could Zach act like everything was normal when everything had changed? Maybe he hoped to let her down gently, but Lia wasn't the kind of person to play dumb. She knew exactly what he was going to say. "I love you but..." or "I have to try to make this work with Violet's mom." Something to that effect. She didn't want to hear it—not a single word.

Soon, Lia reached the park and used the walking trail to calm herself down. The sounds of nature always soothed her soul. However, it was a short-lived experience as the rumble of a car engine sounded behind her.

"Lia, will you please stop and talk to me?"

She turned her head briefly to see Zach following her in his convertible. "I don't want to talk right now. Just give me some space."

"Okay, I will. Just as soon as you tell me what's going on. Will you please sit in the car so we can talk?"

Lia paused on the trail, wiping a few more tears with her sleeve. After a few moments she agreed. "All right, but only for a few minutes." She got into the car and sniffled while turning to look at the backseat. "Where's Violet?"

"Luna offered to watch her."

Lia scoffed and slouched down in the passenger seat with her arms crossed as he drove through town. "I should have known Nana would be involved in this whole scheme."

Zach parked in a small parking lot overlooking Pirate's Cove. With the car off, he turned his attention to her, his face etched with confusion. "Would you mind explaining what scheme you're talking about? Once again, I feel like we're on different pages."

She growled in frustration. "Actually, right now I don't even think we're in the same book! What is there left to explain, Zach? I know what you couldn't tell me over the phone."

His brow arched. "You do?"

She bit her lip, fighting the tears that threatened to burst out of her like a cracked water main. "I met your ex the other day. She was at your house, using your shower. I could understand you might want to make things work for Violet's sake...but that doesn't make this any easier."

"Lia," he said in a gentle tone, capturing her attention. Tears dripped down her nose and cheeks as she waited for the inevitable speech awaiting her. "There's been a misunderstanding. The woman you met yesterday isn't my ex. She's my sister."

Her mind turned to gelatin, wobbling every which direction to grasp his words. "Your what? But...she said Violet was her daughter."

"That's right."

"What?" Lia blinked hard and wiped her tears on her sleeve. "I'm so lost."

He released a weary sigh and explained everything. For the first time, Lia calmed down enough to realize Zach looked completely exhausted with dark circles under his eyes and he was paler than usual. She listened as he explained the story of Emmy's difficult past and how he became Violet's guardian. When he was finished, guilt riddled through her. Poor Zach! He'd been through so much in the last few days, and then he had to defuse her hostile behavior.

She stared straight ahead—her eyes vacant—afraid to look at him in the eye. "Zach, I'm so sorry. I jumped to conclusions when I saw Emmy at the door. Now I feel like such a fool." She rested her head in her hands. "Zach, I'm so sorry. I wouldn't blame you for never wanting to see me again."

"Now, why would I ever want that?"

"Because I didn't trust you."

"I don't blame you for that, but why didn't you call?"

Her lips trembled, but she still refused to look at him. "It's a long story, but my phone is at the bottom of the ocean. Just another one of my classic blunders."

"Lia." His voice was calm and gentle like the ocean breeze coming from the cove, without even a hint of irritation. "Look at me."

She slowly lifted her head and met his gaze. The loving look in his calming blue eyes told her he was sincere and had already forgiven her. Lia never should have questioned his character, but Zach wasn't the kind of man to hold a grudge. However, his forgiveness was only half the battle. "Guess my own insecurities are battling with me again."

"Don't blame yourself, Lia. I think most women wouldn't have known what to think if a strange woman showed up to answer their boyfriend's door."

She grinned, feeling her previous tension drift away. "Yeah, it was quite a jolting experience."

He sighed and rested his head against the headrest. "Was my sister in a bad mood?"

"Yeah, you could say that."

"I'm sorry for my sister's behavior. You might say she doesn't really have a filter. Emmy says everything she thinks, and sometimes the things she thinks aren't very nice."

Lia nodded with a chuckle. "Yeah, I see what you mean. She declared pretty loudly that she wasn't very happy about me ringing the doorbell twice. Then she showed up at the door with only a robe and her hair up in a towel, looking pretty peeved that I'd showed up and wasn't a delivery person."

He shook his head, weariness passing over his face again. "Oh, Lia. No wonder you imagined the worst!"

"No, that's no excuse. I should have trusted you. After all, you've never given me a reason not to."

He reached to run his finger down the curve of her cheek, wiping a rogue tear in the process. "When are you going to stop blaming yourself?"

"When I stop making silly mistakes."

"Come here," he said, leaning closer. When she did as he asked, he rested his forehead against hers and Lia closed her eyes, savoring his closeness. "What's in the past is in the past. It was a misunderstanding. Now we're both on the same page again."

She chuckled softly, but kept her head resting against his. "But are you sure we're in the same book?"

Zach leaned back a little and lifted her chin with his index finger. Before she could say anything else, his lips met hers. She deepened the kiss, and all her anxiety melted away. For a few moments of bliss, nothing mattered. Not misunderstandings, rude sisters, or drowned cell phones at the bottom of the sea.

Only one thing filled Lia's mind. She was falling for Zach Nolan —more deeply than she'd ever fallen for anyone.

When they needed to take a breath, Zach leaned back and smiled at her. "So, are we still on for lunch today? Or has my sister scared you off?"

She grinned back at him. "I'm never going to let anything scare me away from you again."

21

*R*eturning to Zach's house, Lia's heart ratcheted like a tractor motor. She didn't want to go inside and face Emmy's hostility again, but it was necessary. Lia's heart was growing closer to Zach every day, and she didn't want anything to come between them, especially not a rift with his sister.

They let Violet run ahead while making their way onto the porch. Zach weaved his fingers through Lia's and kissed her cheek. "My sister can be moody sometimes, but I'm sure she'll be friendly once she realizes you're my girlfriend."

Lia grinned up at him. "I still can't quite get used to hearing that."

He arched a brow. "I'm assuming you like it though?"

"Of course!" She leaned her head against his shoulder, smiling even bigger.

When they walked in the door, Violet rushed ahead of them into the kitchen. "Aunt Emmy, come meet Daddy's girlfriend. She's in here!"

"Okay, I'm coming." Emmy appeared in the entryway to the kitchen and her eyes widened in shock when she recognized Lia. "Zach, is this your girlfriend? I'm sorry, I had no idea."

He nodded. "Yes, Emmy, I'd like to introduce you to Natalia Diaz."

"Please, just call me Lia for short," she said, extending her hand.

"I go by a shortened version of my name, too. My full name is really Emerson."

"What a beautiful name."

"Thank you." Emmy shook her hand with a sheepish look on her face. "I'm so sorry about the other day. I was in one of my moods."

"That's fine. I completely understand. I can get in a bad mood sometimes too." Lia's shoulders relaxed, realizing what had happened yesterday had been a misunderstanding. Emmy turned out to be a warm and welcoming person after all.

After lunch, Lia sat on the back deck with Emmy, watching Violet and Zach collect eggs from the nesting boxes. There were a few chickens in the boxes, and Zach held the lid open so Violet could pet each one of them. When they were done, he lifted Violet onto his shoulders and pretended to be a pony as she used imaginary reins to steer him around the garden.

Lia laughed while watching them. "They make quite a pair, don't they?"

Emmy nodded, but her smile left. "Yeah, they do."

She wondered what changed Emmy's moods so quickly and tried to bring back some lightness to the conversation. "So, Zach told me you came here from Florida. Do you like it there?"

Emmy shrugged. "It's okay, but it will be better once I can afford this nicer apartment I want to rent with my boyfriend." She paused before looking at her again. "Did Zach also tell you I'm planning on taking Violet with me?"

Lia gulped, trying not to reveal her shock over the matter. No wonder Zach had looked so tired that morning. "No, he didn't mention it."

"I'm surprised. We haven't stopped arguing about it since I

brought up the idea." Emmy shook her head with a frown. "I know what you must think of me. That I'm cruel and heartless."

"No, I could never think that, and I'm sure Zach doesn't think so either."

She sighed. "Maybe not, but he sure doesn't trust me enough to let me spend time alone with Violet."

"He'll come around with time if you work to earn his trust. He's only trying to protect Violet and do what's best for her."

Emmy turned her attention back to Violet, who was helping Zach fill the goat feeders with alfalfa. She sighed, and a waved of sadness passed over her face. "You're right. I guess I can't complain that he's such a devoted guardian for Violet. He's given her a life I never could have provided...not in a million years. Zach has always had a heart of gold. Whatever he tends grows and flourishes. But me..." She shook her head. "I can't even keep a houseplant alive. I'm a lost cause."

Lia studied Emmy for the first time, seeing a bit of herself in the younger woman's eyes. She'd never had an addiction, but she did know what it felt like to fail to meet other people's expectations. "From one lost sparrow to another, there's no such thing as a lost cause. I came here to stay with my nana because I was ashamed to tell my family I'd lost my job. My brother and sisters are all married with kids. I'm the only single one...also the only one without a stable job. My dad doesn't say it out loud, but I can tell I'm disappointing him."

"I know how that feels."

Lia nodded. "But when I came here, Nana helped me realize that God still sees me and cares about me. He finds lost sparrows and helps them discover a new way to fly."

Emmy's eyes clouded with tears. "Do you really think so? I've been clean for a year, but it still feels like my life is a mess. I wonder if I even deserve to try and create a relationship with Violet after I abandoned her."

Before speaking again, Lia said a silent prayer that she'd say the right thing to help instill a little hope in Emmy's discouraged soul. "I believe God can do miraculous things. He can change and mold us into new creations. Your brother has a special bond with Violet, but I think she needs you in her life, too. Her world won't be complete if both of you aren't in it."

Right on cue, Violet came running over with a big grin on her face. "Auntie Emmy, the baby bunnies have their eyes open!"

"They do?" Emmy smiled and wiped her moist cheeks.

"Yeah, do you want to see them?"

"I'd love to."

Violet's excited blue eyes met Lia's. "Do you want to come too?"

Lia shook her head. "Maybe later. I'm finishing my iced tea. You can take Aunt Emmy to see them right now."

Emmy mouthed a quick thank you before heading off with Violet hand in hand.

Ringing startled Kendall into consciousness. She reached for her phone blindly in the dark, dropping it on the floor and scrambling to pick it up again. When she finally gripped it, the phone stopped ringing. The screen lit up, revealing it was two in the morning and Tiff had been calling. Kendall's heart leapt into her throat. A middle of the night call wasn't a good sign.

"Please God," she prayed out loud. "Not Tyler. Please not Tyler!"

She called Tiff back, her heart pounding so hard she could barely hear the phone ringing. When Tiff's voicemail picked up, she growled in frustration and hung up. She tried again after a few seconds, and she finally picked up. When Tiff's voice came through the speaker, she was overcome with emotion. "They found him, Kendall."

"A...Alive?" she managed, her voice quivering.

"Yes, he's alive and has been taken to the military hospital with the rest of the men in his squadron."

"Is he injured?"

Tiff paused, and it seemed to take an eternity for her to answer. "They couldn't tell me much, but I know he's stable."

Kendall sat on the bed as tears of joy and concern flowed down her cheeks. There were too many emotions coursing through her to decipher how she really felt. She had to remind herself of the most important thing. He was alive. They would deal with her other concerns later.

"Kendall, are you okay?"

"Yeah, I'm fine," she responded robotically, stuck in a dream-like state. After a week of turmoil, Tyler was safe. It didn't feel real yet. "Thank you for calling," she managed.

Tiff started to say something else, but a low beep interrupted. Kendall brought the phone away from her ear to look at the screen. An unknown number was scrolling across the screen. This early in the morning, she knew it had to be important.

"Tiff, I'm going to have to let you go. Someone is beeping in."

"Okay, talk to you soon."

Kendall switched to the other call and said hello. At first, the person's voice was garbled and fuzzy, but a few moments later the voice came through loud and clear. The most beautiful voice she'd ever heard. "Kendall, can you hear me?"

"Tyler?" She bit her lip to keep from bursting into tears.

"It's me, babe. I'm okay." His voice sounded overcome as well.

"I was so worried, but I felt like God just wanted me to keep praying."

"He heard you. It looked bad there for a while. I wasn't sure if we'd make it, but He was there every step of the way."

"Praise the Lord! Are you sure you're okay? Tiff said they were taking you to the hospital and..."

"I'm a little dehydrated and exhausted, but fine," he reassured. "The whole squadron is fine actually. Well, I take that back. We did have one casualty…"

"Oh, Tyler. I'm sorry."

"…my prosthetic leg," he finished.

Her brow furrowed in confusion. "What?"

He let out a chuckle—the best sound she'd heard in a long time. "The leg took the hit. It's toast, but I'm fine, although I have to hobble around on crutches till they find me a replacement."

They both laughed and cried until Kendall's cheek muscles ached. "I love you, Tyler. So much it hurts."

"Me too. I wish I could hold you in my arms right now, but we'll only have to wait about a week. I'll be back stateside by then. Boy, do I have a story to tell you when I get there."

"I can't wait to hear it."

Tears of joy rolled down her cheeks as they said goodbye, and hope filled her heart anew. In only a week her Merriweather Hero would be home for good.

a smile bloomed on Lia's lips as she parked in front of Nana's apartment building. Zach's SUV was already there. Was it already Wednesday? The work week at the clinic had been hectic, with Kendall gone off and on. Lia was needed full time again to help Alicia, but that also made it go by quicker than usual. With Tyler Banner coming home at the end of the week, the residents were planning a grand welcome home party. Kendall and Tiff were a big part of the planning process. She was still amazed Kendall's boyfriend had been found safe and was coming home. The miracle from God was definitely something worth celebrating.

After coming down the path, she saw Nana, Emmy and Violet on the porch playing a game of Rummy on the outdoor table. Nana's doctor had allowed her to remove the boot, and she looked happier than she had in weeks. Lia offered all three of them a warm greeting. When Violet finished her turn, she ran down the steps and leapt into her arms. "Lia, I won two times!"

"Wow, good job." She hugged the little girl close before setting her feet back on the ground.

She looked up at Nana, who gave her a knowing smile. "Zach is with Jace, building the raised garden beds.

"Thanks. I'll go up there and see if I can help with anything."

Arriving at the build location of the community gardens, Lia found her surroundings swarming with activity. Most of the raised garden beds were constructed and placed in uniform rows. The few that weren't completed had people pounding nails into the wood to keep them in place. A large dump truck sat nearby, and the men were shoveling it into the completed beds. There was another truck waiting nearby with bricks for the stone path around the gardens.

Zach smiled when he saw her and set his shovel aside. He gave her a brief kiss before taking her hand and leading her around to look at everything. "Amazing how fast something can be accomplished when you have a billionaire sponsor, huh?"

She nodded. "Amazing. I'm so happy your dream is coming true, Zach. This is going to be a great resource for the community."

"I hope so."

"What can I help with?"

He scratched his head. "Well, after the dirt goes in, I have some skids of nursery plants that need to be planted." He pointed in the direction of the plants on foldable tables off to the side. "There are trowels and fertilizer over there too."

She grinned at him. "Sure, I can do that, although I can't promise much. I don't have much of a green thumb."

He held her in his arms again, pausing to kiss her forehead. "There's not much to it. I'll show you how to get started when we're ready for that step." His attention drifted to Jace, who was over talking to one of the contractors Luc had hired. He turned back to Lia and kissed her cheek. "I'll be back soon."

She watched him walk away, admiring the way his tank top showed off his arm muscles. He usually wore polo or button-down shirts, and this was the first time she'd seen him doing hard labor outside, besides taking care of the animals at his house. Lia enjoyed seeing this industrial side of him.

She turned away to study the nursery plants on the table when her new phone made a foreign sound from her pocket, startling her. It had only arrived by mail yesterday and she was still getting use to the ring tone. Lia calmed herself and took it out, staring at the number scrolling across the screen. Why would her old boss be calling? As all the hurt and resentment came flooding over her, Lia considered not answering, but out of pure curiosity, she did. "Hi Marcela. It's been a while."

"Hi Lia. I'm sorry to call you out of the blue."

You had me fired out of the blue, Lia thought to herself, but held her tongue. She'd changed since working for Marcela—changed for the better. Although she had the urge to spew her anger like lava, in the end she knew it wasn't worth it and wouldn't change anything. "Can I help you with something?" Lia offered instead, reining back her temper.

Marcela sighed on the other end of the line. It was obvious whatever she had to say wasn't easy for her. "The fact is, Lia, since you've been gone, things haven't been that great around here. We've lost some of our staff to a rival magazine."

"Oh, really. I'm sorry to hear that."

There was a long pause before Marcela continued. "The reason I'm calling is we'd like you to come into the office on Friday afternoon. We have a proposal for you."

Lia started biting her nails, remembering the welcome party was also on Friday. "I'm not sure I can make it. I have a prior commitment."

"Believe me, Lia. This is a meeting you won't want to pass up."

She let out a sigh of resignation. Lia had thought she'd rather eat a wasabi flavored ice cream cone than ever return to her old job at the magazine, but being a curious person by heart, could she live with the "what ifs' if she didn't go and hear them out?

She ran her fingers through her hair while glancing at Zach in the distance. She'd gone back and forth in her mind so many times about whether she should stay on the Independence Islands or go back to her apartment in the city. Now the conflict between her heart and her head had come to a breaking point. If they offered Lia her dream job, would she be able to resist?

"Okay," she finally answered. "I'll come and listen to the proposal. What time should I be there?"

On Friday morning, Zach woke up at six on the dot. Having volunteered to be at the church at nine to help with setting up for Tyler Banner's welcome home party, he wanted to get an early start. He hadn't slept well, thinking about Lia's conference at her old job. Would she be enticed to stay on the mainland by a higher paying job?

He rubbed the sleep out of his eyes while coming into the kitchen to put on a pot of coffee. However, the smell of a fresh brew told him someone had already put on the coffee for him. Emmy sat at the kitchen island, already sipping on a cup of the steaming liquid. "You're up early."

She offered him a bright smile—a rare sight to see from his sister—especially so early in the morning. "So are you."

He looked down, noticing the packed duffle bag resting by her feet. "Emmy, what's going on?"

Her strong façade crumbled and her lips quivered. "I wanted to thank you, Zach. Thank you for giving me a second chance when I didn't deserve one. I'm sorry I've been such a pain."

He gulped hard. "I'd never think of you like that. You're my sister and I love you, no matter what."

She nodded as tears dripped down her face. "I know, and I love you, too, even if I don't say it as often as I should." She wiped her face. "I'll have to catch the ferry soon, so I wanted to make sure you knew that before I leave."

Zach's legs trembled as he sat on the stool next to her. "Where will you go?"

"Back to Miami. This week, after watching you with Violet, I know you're what's best for her."

"She needs you, too. Don't forget that."

Emmy nodded, wiping another tear. "Lia said the same thing, and I know you're both right. I want to have her in my life, but I don't think I'm ready to be a mother to her. Guess I'll have to settle for being the cool aunt."

"That's fine, but please stay, Emmy. Give her a chance to get to know you better. Earning a child's trust takes time."

She nodded. "That's why I'm not leaving for good. I need to go home and talk to Axel. I need to get some things in order. Do some soul searching, you might say. I...I'm not sure when I'll be coming back."

Zach nodded, fighting tears himself. "Can't you stay here, or get an apartment on Hopper? I know all the quiet is hard to get used to at first, but you could live a good life here and see Violet whenever you want."

Emmy looked out the window, her eyes focused on something far in the distance. "I might do that someday, but right now I just need some time. Lia said God looks out for lost sparrows. I need to find out if that's true. Maybe with time, He'll lead me right where I'm supposed to be."

He managed a trembling smile, finally giving in to his sister's strong-willed nature. "You have always done things in your own timing. Haven't you?"

Emmy nodded, grinning with her chin lifted high. "Sure have, brother. That's why you love me so much."

"Sure do." Zach leaned forward and pulled his sister into a hug, silently praying for God to keep her safe and bring her back to Sparrow soon. "How are you getting to the ferry? Can I drive you to the slip?"

She leaned back and grinned at him. "No. The walk will do me some good. My feet have never failed me before. I'll catch a cab after reaching the mainland."

Zach protested, but the determined look in Emmy's eyes caused him to stop. Once his sister made up her mind about something, there was very little chance of talking her out of it. "Will you wait until Violet wakes up? I know she'll want to say bye."

Emmy shook her head, her eyes tearing up again. "No, please let her sleep. That will just make things harder. Please tell her I'll send her letters when I get back to Florida. We could be like pen pals. After all, she'll be going to school soon and learning to read and write."

"I'm sure she'll love that idea."

She gathered her duffle bag and slung the strap over one shoulder. "Well, that's my cue. Thanks for everything, Zach."

He put his hand out. "Wait just a sec. I have something for you." He rushed upstairs and came down a few minutes later, holding a Bible with a little wear and tear around the spine. "This was one of Mom's. I think you should have it. It's a study Bible with devotions. It also has a check tucked inside the cover. That should help with living expenses until you find a good job."

She shook her head, tears brimming. "Oh, Zach, you should keep the Bible. That's something of hers you treasure, I'm sure. And the money...I never should have asked for it in the first place. It was selfish of me."

He shook his head and pushed it into her hands, refusing to take no for an answer. "She would have wanted you to have it. As far as the money goes, I'd feel much better knowing you have something to fall back on. Consider it a loan if you want."

She arched an amused eyebrow. "A loan you'll refuse to let me pay back."

His lips quirked upward. "Something like that." He hugged her again. "Take care of yourself, sis."

"You too."

With a few more tears, they parted ways, and Zach watched his sister walk out the door. He watched until she disappeared around a bend in the road. Watching her go broke his heart like the first time they were separated from each other, but he felt God mending the wound as well. A peace filled him, believing this wouldn't be another long absence. He would bring Emmy back when the time was right.

Back in her Savannah apartment, Lia tried on three different business outfits, finally settling on a dark gray pencil skirt and tailored blazer, accented with a purple blouse. Thankfully, the majority of her work clothes were still in her apartment, so she had plenty to choose from. Lia had left the islands earlier than she needed to, so she'd have plenty of time to prepare for her afternoon meeting.

She turned at a different angle to study her outfit one more time before crossing to her closet to select a matching pair of heels and a clutch. It was her power outfit—at least that's what she called it when she first bought it a year ago when her job at the magazine had been her life.

"I'm back," she said to her reflection with a confident smile. Almost as soon as the words came out of her mouth, Lia's smile dissolved into a frown. Deep down, she liked the idea of success and more money. It represented a life of both respect and comfort. However, did she really want to morph into that kind of life again? Her life for the past month with Nana had been so peaceful and eye opening. She'd learned life wasn't about having it all. It was about living a meaningful life God had planned for her. Now at the crossroads, Lia struggled to choose the right path.

Someone knocked on the door and Lia looked through the peephole and recoiled seeing it was her sister, Mia. She was standing with her hand braced on her hip, with a scowl painted on her face. "Lia, are you in there?"

"Hold on." She opened the door and let her in. "Sorry Mia. I wasn't expecting you. How did you know I was here?"

"Well, I've been trying to call you all week."

"I'm sorry. My phone is at the bottom of the ocean. I just got a new one and I haven't caught up on voicemails yet."

Mia's mouth hinged open for a moment before she closed it and shook her head. "Well, I'd love to hear that story, but we don't have time. Anyway, I finally gave up and called Nana, but she wouldn't tell me anything except you've been staying with her for the month. Said it was your place to tell me the rest. So, I came here to find out the truth. What's going on Lia? I know something's up!"

Sighing, Lia sat on the arm of the couch. "I got fired from my job, so Nana invited me to stay for a few months so I could figure things out."

"Oh my!" Mia leaned against the wall—her eyes wide.

"Please, just hear me out and try not to overreact. I've changed so much since spending time on the Islands...and I even met someone." A spontaneous smile spread across her face. "I really like him."

Her sister groaned and her expression morphed into a grimace. "I can't believe this is happening. Not now. It's too soon."

Lia furrowed her brow. "What's so wrong with me falling in love? Really, Mia, I hoped you wouldn't be so judgmental."

"No, it's not that." She held her stomach and groaned again. "I think I'm going into labor!"

"You're what?"

Water dripped onto the floor, and Mia's eyes grew even wider. "Lia, I need to go to the hospital. Now!"

She gulped hard. "Okay, don't panic," she said, really trying to convince herself not to panic. Lia held onto her sister's arm, leading her toward the door and grabbing her purse on the way. "Let's get to my car. Everything's going to be fine."

"What about Jaime?" her sister asked. "He wanted to be there for the birth. He's my coach, too!"

"We'll call him on the way. Come on. Let's go."

23

*L*ia held the perfect little bundle in her arms, marveling how someone so tiny could evoke such strong emotions. The little girl was so precious and somehow put things into perspective. "She's beautiful, Mia. Just like you. Have you thought of a name yet?"

Mia offered an exhausted smile. "I was thinking of naming her after you. Peyton Lia Cadman. What do you think?"

Lia smiled through happy tears. "I think it sounds perfect." She kissed little Peyton on the forehead and handed her back to Mia. "What a wonderful gift it was to see her birth."

"Thank you, Lia. I don't know what I would have done without you. I hope I didn't make you miss anything important. You're all dressed up."

"Just something about a job."

Mia gasped. "I'm sorry. I hope they'll be able to reschedule."

Lia shrugged. "It's not going to be a right fit for me anyway."

Her sister lifted a curious eyebrow. "Does this have anything to do with the guy you've fallen in love with?"

Lia felt heat rising to her cheeks. "Who said I'd fallen in love?"

"You did."

She furrowed her brow, ready to set the record straight. "No, I never said..." Lia paused, playing back the last few hours like an old-fashion projector. It was all hazy and mixed up, but she had said it and it was true. She did love Zach.

Mia grinned. "Does this guy make you happy?"

"Yes, I don't think I've ever been happier in my life." Lia's heart was so full of joy she thought she'd burst. She looked at her watch, seeing it was four in the afternoon. She'd completely missed the meeting, but she didn't care anymore. "Oh, the party on Merriweather! I completely forgot."

Mia's eyebrow arched. "Is this guy going to be there?"

"Um, yes, but I can't leave you here."

Her sister aimed a stubborn look in her direction. "Yes, you can. Jaimie is ten minutes away. Get out of here."

Lia hugged her sister, careful not to squish her niece. "Thank you for understanding."

"Of course. I only want you to be happy, and I'm glad you are. Nana did tell me a little more than I let on." Mia winked in her direction.

Lia put her hands on her hips in mock annoyance. "Well, you two are co-conspirators then."

Mia laughed as Lia gathered her purse to leave. "And proud of it, sis"

Zach stood off to the side of the crowd at the Merriweather Church fellowship hall with Violet and Luna standing with him. He checked his phone for the umpteenth time. Lia's appointment had been at three, so she should have been back by now. It grew more crowded as the minutes ticked by. Zach was sure even if Lia did walk in, he wouldn't be able to see her.

"She'll be here," Luna reassured, noticing his apprehension.

"I know," Zach said and smiled at her. However, his mind kept playing cruel tricks on him. Did her delayed arrival mean she decided to take the job? He'd tried his best to be supportive, but the raw truth remained—he didn't want her to move away.

When it was time for Tyler to arrive, the room grew quiet. Zach watched intently as the Marine came in, still dressed in his uniform and using crutches to get around. He waved and greeted everyone warmly, but it was clear what his intentions were when he made a b-line for Kendall Mulligan. They shared a long passionate kiss as the crowd in the room clapped and cheered. After that, he hugged his sister, Tiff, and her three kids. Happy tears flowed like rain as the family reunited.

Zach pulled Violet up on his shoulders so she could see better as Tyler and his family moved to a small podium with a microphone stand. The Marine took the microphone from the stand and smiled at the crowd, clearly overcome. "Thank you for the warm welcome home. All those months overseas, the thing that helped me sleep at night was thinking of home. I hoped I'd come back and see the same people I grew up with—this wonderful community who has always supported me and my family. Thank you for your constant prayers and support. He turned to his family on the platform. To my sister Tiff and her family, I love you all. Your letters and prayers helped me keep going. And to my wonderful girlfriend Kendall, thank you for your unwavering faith and support. I know for a fact God answered your prayers. He kept me alive and brought me home." Kendall came closer, and they shared another kiss as the crowd clapped and cheered again.

Zach continued listening to Tyler's speech but looked around one more time to see if he could find Lia in the crowd. He was about to give up when he spotted her coming through a side door. She looked radiant in her purple blouse and gray skirt, yet the fear in his heart remained.

She looked around for a few moments before seeing him and coming over. "What did I miss?"

His heart pounded as he put Violet down to give his shoulders a break. "Only the beginning."

"Sorry I'm late."

"That's all right. You're here now." The suspense was killing him, but he'd have to wait to ask her about the meeting until later.

Up on the stage something was happening, and the crowd was even louder in response. Looking up, he saw Tyler turning to face Kendall. "Kendall Mulligan, I can't imagine spending my life with anyone but you. You've brought a light into my life I never thought I would find. Even through the hard times when things seemed hopeless, you remained strong and kept faith we would make it to this moment. If it weren't for these crutches, I'd be down on one knee but I can't delay any longer. I've waited fifteen long months to ask you this question. Will you marry me?"

Kendall nodded while wiping happy tears from her eyes and moved toward the microphone. "Yes. Of course, I will."

After the party began winding down, Zach invited Lia outside. Nana offered to watch Violet so they could have some alone time. As they sat on a bench outside the church, Lia's heart drummed in her chest as Zach turned to face her. "I wasn't sure if you were coming or not."

She let out a nervous chuckle. "Honestly, I didn't know if I'd make it or not."

"What happened?"

"I don't even know where to start. Let's just say it was a very eventful trip to the mainland."

Zach's smile faded. "Lia, you don't have to be afraid to tell me if you accepted the job. I'm happy for you. Even if you have to live on the mainland, we can still see each other on the weekends. We can make this work."

"Hey," she said, touching his cheek to stop him. "I didn't even go to the meeting."

"You didn't?"

"No, I didn't." Lia grinned and pressed her forehead against his, trying to calm him like he'd calmed her recently. "The job wasn't right for me...and there's one other reason."

"What's that?"

"Isn't it obvious Zach Nolan? I love you."

"And I love you." He let out a shaky sigh of relief and pulled her into his embrace, kissing her until they were breathless. He leaned back to outline her cheek with his finger. "So, you're staying here?"

She grinned before kissing him again. "When a lost sparrow finds a home, she'd have to be a fool to leave it."

ABOUT THE AUTHOR

Rachel Skatvold is a Christian author and homeschooling mom from the Midwest. She enjoys writing inspirational romance and encouraging blogs. Rachel completed her first series, the Riley Family Legacy Novellas in 2014, and is now working on the Hart Ranch Series, set in the Montana wilderness, and the Ladies of Ardena Series, set in medieval times. She is also a contributing author in the Whispers in Wyoming, Brides of Pelican Rapids, and Independence Islands Series. Other than writing, some of her hobbies include singing, reading, and camping in the great outdoors with her husband and two young sons. You can find more information about Rachel and her books on her website: **www.rachelskatvold.com**.

f facebook.com/rachelskatvoldauthor
🐦 twitter.com/rachelskatvold
BB bookbub.com/profile/rachel-skatvold

ALSO BY RACHEL SKATVOLD

CONTEMPORARY ROMANCE

Independence Islands

Her Merriweather Hero

The Elnora Monet

Hooper Safe Haven

Stranded on Sparrow

Riley Family Legacy

Beauty Within

Beauty Unveiled

Beauty Restored

Billionaires and Debutantes

Chasing a Christmas Carol

CONTEMPORARY WESTERN ROMANCE

Hart Ranch

Escaping Reality

Chasing Embers

Growing Roots

Whispers in Wyoming

Guardian of her Heart

A Forgetful Heart

Melodies of the Heart

A Searching Heart

Lessons from the Heart

Patient Hearts

HISTORICAL WESTERN ROMANCE

Brides of Pelican Rapids

Caroline's Quilt

Vivian's Morning Star

MEDIEVAL ROMANCE

Ladies of Ardena

Lady Airell's Choice

Lady Reagan's Quest

Lady Fiona's Refuge

Lady Gwyneth's Hope

BOOKS IN THE SPARROW ISLAND SERIES

Finding a Memory (Book One) by Chautona Havig

Blended Lives (Book Two) by Melissa Wardwell

Sweet Rivals (Book Three) by Kari Trumbo

Stranded on Sparrow (Book Four) by Rachel Skatvold

From Shore to Shore (Book Five) by Tabitha Bouldin

Rebuilding Hearts (Book Six) by Carolyn Miller

FROM SHORE TO SHORE

SPARROW ISLAND BOOK FIVE SNEAK PEEK

TABITHA BOULDIN

A brand-new adventure on a clean horizon. Bree Jamison dusted off her hands and stepped from the *Acadia*'s deck to bleached dock boards. Her sea legs complained, sending her listing sideways a half step. She jerked upright before her jelly legs plunged her off the dock. Not that she'd mind a swim—rather looking forward to it—but not quite yet. Davy Jones' locker would wait another day. She'd never been a fan of pirates, but she couldn't argue with beauty. Of all the places she'd lived, Sparrow Island won the award for most memorable. Even though she'd yet to truly live there. Remote. Picturesque. Perfect. The next six months would be a breeze.

Planting her hands on her hips, she turned and scanned the place she'd call home. Endless ocean banked by billowy clouds and not a boat in sight. Except for the two-seater craft bobbing alongside their larger research vessel, captainless but well docked.

Damien, her diving partner of the last year and fellow marine biologist, brushed a hand through his golden hair and tossed her the *Acadia*'s line. She twisted the rope around the piling and quickly threw a double hitch around the cleat.

Damien offered her a smile that could charm a shark. Goodness. Who needed a defibrillator with smiles like that? She shook off the feeling.

"All right there, Bree?"

"Never better." Especially if he kept smiling like that. At her. *Stop it. Remember what happened last time you let a gorgeous smile make decisions for you.*

They followed the same routine for the second line, securing their boat as second nature as breathing. Damien tossed her satchel at her feet and followed, landing on the dock with a graceful thud. "Come on. Wait till you see the beach house. It's perfect."

"Better than the place in Barbados?"

"You had to bring that up, didn't you?" Laughter rippled through the salty air. "I mess up one time and you can't let me forget it."

"If it wasn't for that mistake, I'd still be wondering if you were human." Bree matched his stride, swinging the satchel over her shoulder. The dock creaked, waves lapping the piling and sending the *Acadia* bobbing against her lines.

He slipped on a pair of Ray Bans that reflected the beach back at Bree when she glanced his way. His voice took on the smooth glide of pride. "That's me. Damien the Destroyer. Sent to Earth to swindle beautiful women."

And swindle them he would. Not out of money or valuables, but of their hearts. Their love. All but hers. Four women in the last year they'd worked together. Damien loved and discarded women the way many tossed aside disposable coffee cups.

Bree's heels sank into soft earth. Sand churned with each step, the spray of fiery particles burning her calves. Beach stretched out on either side, disappearing far into the distance as the island curved, hiding her secrets. No shade to protect the sand from the blistering sun. Sweat carved a path down her back. *Should have taken the swim.* She needed the water, the blissful quiet.

"You wouldn't believe the sweet deal I got on our house." Damien chattered, arrogantly unaware of any tension or turmoil. "I could have bought the place for less than a year's salary. Almost did."

That knocked Bree out of her island stupor. "You're leaving?" Great. Just what she needed. To lose another partner.

"Could have bought. Pay attention to the words I say, and you'll have less chance to misunderstand." He knocked his shoulder against hers, a playful action with no more ardor than a clown fish and its anemone. "I'm not ready to hang up my flippers yet."

No. Doing that would mean settling down. Something they'd both sworn never to do and a decision that made them excellent partners who flitted around the globe in six-month spans to dive, document, and survey the ocean corals. Which is why they made perfect sense as a couple. Like minded. Similar goals. Perfect match. Except Damien loved falling in love.

"I thought our captain was supposed to meet us at the dock." She shuffled through the last stretch of sand, relieved when a stand of Loblolly pine cast a welcome shade over her heated body.

"He's meeting us at the house. Said he'd make sure the fridge was stocked and no rodents were making nests in the corners."

Staving off a shiver, Bree kicked a small stone, sending it flying to thwack against a tree trunk. The childish gesture tickled an old memory of laughter. Stepping between two pines, the house popped into view as though it had been hiding behind a curtain like a child, waiting to jump out and shout its arrival.

Butter yellow exterior and a silver roof dappled with light drew her toward the wide porch wrapping across the front with glass double doors planted square in the middle of the house. Her first step was tentative, testing the strength and durability of the worn stairs. Bleached to a dull gray, they held her weight without a creak.

A shadow dropped over her, deeper than those cast by the trees, and a voice rumbled, gravely and dark. "Well, well. We meet again."

Bree's head snapped up, her gaze finding the chocolate-colored eyes of the man she met during her exploratory excursion to the Independence Islands so many months ago. "Didn't know I'd made such a lasting impression."

Damien scooted past her, cutting her off from the intensity of the stranger's smile. "You two know each other?"

"We met when I came over to scout the islands for coral. He saved me from a murderous parrot."

"It's not every day a stranger stumbles into a wedding party." He chuckled, the sound as warm as his eyes had been that day. "Until you showed up again at the Christmas festival, I thought I'd imagined you."

Ah, yes. The festival where she'd browsed stalls and wheedled information from the locals about coral reefs and diving locations.

"She's a wily one. Don't get your hopes up on her sticking around this time either. Bree doesn't *do* permanent." Damien waved his hand toward the house. "Just the mention of buying a house and putting down roots makes her squirm."

Though her jaw tightened at Damien's casual offering of her personal beliefs, she didn't refute his claims. Roots. Blech. Who wanted to stay in one place, staid and immovable? Not her. That's why she loved the ocean. So much they didn't know. A million new things to discover and explore. Never the same. Never boring.

"We going inside or standing out here until we turn into dried out husks?" Shouldering her bag, she strode toward the door, wrenching it open and accepting the burst of air conditioning. Her skin cooled, drawing a smattering of goosebumps across her arms when her damp shirt rustled across her back.

Open and spacious, the living area welcomed her with hues of cream and beige. A basket filled with fruit rested in the center of the glass table, bright reds and sunny yellows promising a welcome relief from the sudden hunger pinching her stomach.

Footsteps sounded at her back. Bree moved aside, allowing the two men to enter the house. She propped a hip against the counter and settled her arms loosely across her stomach.

Their captain offered a hand. "Cooper Carmichael. Nice to meet you...officially." His head cocked to the side, the teasing hint of a smile pulling one side of his mouth.

Bree shook his hand, the rough skin a testament to hard work. "When can we dive?"

"Straight to business. As usual." Damien kicked off his shoes and flopped onto the couch with a yawn. "We have six months on this speck of land. There's no rush."

Interesting. Damien never slacked off from his work.

"Tell me about this meeting you two had." He snagged a banana from the bowl and peeled it with precision.

"Not much to tell." Bree shrugged, her gaze searching Cooper's face. "I stopped on Merriweather to scout around. Someone mentioned an old lady who would probably know the local history."

"Miss Evelyn." Cooper cut in, the overhead light illuminating the scruff of beard across his chin. He took up the story, facing Bree with a look of amusement. "My sister was getting married. Miss Evelyn is her husband's grandmother. Bree arrived as they were leaving. Out of nowhere, a parrot dive bombs the wedding party, coming specifically for Bree."

"I would think you liked birds. What with them being able to flit from place to place as you do." Damien's careless appraisal sounded fair, but something about his tone drew tension into the air.

Bree shouldered her bag and pushed off from the counter. Damien thought he knew her. Felt confident enough to share her life with a stranger. An oversight she needed to correct. Later. "I'm going for a swim." Anger rippled beneath the surface, drawing heat up her neck. Damien never met a stranger, but that didn't mean she felt the same.

"Mind if I check out the boat before I leave?" Cooper sent a glance between her and Damien as though uncertain which of them had the power to grant permission.

"Go ahead." Bree waved her hand toward the door and the path leading to the beach. "Give me a couple minutes to change and I'll walk you down."

"I think I'll head into town. There *is* a town, isn't there?"

Cooper swiveled to face Damien. "Depends on what you're looking to find. If it's entertainment, you'll need to head up to Mimosa. The other islands are locals only, with you two as an exception for your research. We have a few amenities."

Escaping the room, Bree blew out a long breath to expel the rise in temperature before it could take root. Down a short hallway, she found two rooms across from each other with a bathroom at the end of the hall. Nothing they hadn't encountered before. She took the room on the right, facing the ocean though all she saw through the windows were trees. Silence settled around her, that same peaceful oblivion she found beneath the ocean.

Her bag landed on the bed with a soft plop, cushioned by an off-white comforter. Pillows covered half the bed, an array of soft blues and grays.

She took her time changing into a simple one-piece bathing suit and finding a towel in the moderate bathroom. Cooper's voice sounded from the living room, followed by the slide of the door and a heavy sigh from Damien. Whatever crab had pinched her partner, it wouldn't last. Nothing with him ever did, except for the job.

Damien lounged against the wall, apparently waiting for her. "Sorry." He ruffled both hands through his hair. "I don't mean to talk about you like that."

"I get it." She strode around him. "We've spent too many hours together in close quarters. Get out of here. Blow off some steam, or whatever it is you do." She wheeled around and planted a finger in his chest. "But when you come back, I expect this to be gone. No more of whatever that was. You've made it clear that you're not part of my personal life, so stop treating my life like blood you can toss overboard to chum the water."

"You got it, boss." He fingered a mini salute.

He didn't smile, a sure sign he'd taken her words to heart.

Bree backed into the living room. What made sense in theory often fell apart in real life, as the last few minutes proved. No relationship was worth that kind of trouble. If they didn't leave because of a bout of conscious on how their life would be perfect with another partner, they turned, throwing her to the sharks.

Better to travel the globe, never settling, than to be trapped in one place long enough to watch as they walked away. *Just keep swimming.* Dory's motto. One aimed toward perseverance, but Bree took it as a reminder to never let emotional attachments sink in their hooks.

Made in the USA
Middletown, DE
11 May 2022

65530246R00111